COLLISION

COLLISION

DEBRA M. COOPER

Jones Media Publishing
10645 N. Tatum Blvd. Ste. 200-166
Phoenix, AZ 85028
www.JonesMediaPublishing.com

Printed in the United States of America

ISBN: 978-1-945849-02-2 paperback

ACKNOWLEDGEMENT

Because God is the source of all that is good, I have only to thank Him. He gave me the best possible husband, Joe Hoyt, and son, Zack Howland. In addition, throughout the years, He has blessed me with the most exceptional women friends, who have filled my life with joy, love, and importantly, laughter.

In this particular instance, I thank Him for giving me a profound appreciation for words and the ability to use them well. .

CONTENTS

PART
I

AUGUST, 2002

I

THE YELLOW CAB SCREECHED TO a stop at the curb and the rear door swung wide. John Larken climbed out onto the busy sidewalk and sped through the sliding glass doors of the San Diego airport. Inside, he hurried to the American Air counter and fell into line behind a handful of other passengers.

Shifting from foot to foot, John plunged a hand through his disheveled hair. He had depended on that alarm clock for years. It had never let him down. Then, today of all days? What time was it, anyway? He glanced at his wrist. Bare. He had forgotten his watch. He scanned the terminal, and found nothing. In the world of aviation where time was money, clocks should be everywhere. He tapped the toe of one shoe on the floor. *Seriously, could this line move any slower?*

From behind the counter, the ticket agent did a quick evaluation of the man who had just walked in. He was tall and well-built with slightly mussed chestnut brown hair--probably in the mid-thirties. More important, he possessed that raw, masculine appeal that Cara found so attractive. She gave the situation some thought as she executed the standard check-in procedure with the next passenger. Her best friend, Annie, worked at the United Airlines counter. She was always telling Cara to be more assertive and flirtatious with good looking male passengers. The strategy sure worked for Annie. She had dates practically every night of the week.

Cara bit the inside of her lip and completed the transaction with the current customer. She stole another peek at the man as he drew near. Damn, he was cute, even if he did look a little stressed out. Cara decided she was going to go for it.

The current customer walked away and the man rushed forward. Cara's gaze skipped the coffee-brown eyes altogether and went straight to what mattered—the bulging asset tucked securely inside a crisp pair of Levi's. Not bad, not bad at all. Encouraged, she flashed her most bewitching smile and inclined her head just the precise amount to cause her long black hair to drape over one shoulder. "Good morning."

"Yes, hello."

She fluttered her eyelashes and allowed her French manicured fingernails to graze his skin as she accepted his ticket. "And what is your destination today?"

"I'm going to New York City. Am I too late? Did I make it on time?"

"Now don't you worry one little bit." She playfully patted the knuckles of his outstretched hand. "The flight is going to be a few minutes delayed. You have plenty of time."

The man's shoulders relaxed, a small sigh escaped his lips.

"Are you traveling alone today?"

He gave a quick nod of assent.

She leaned closer to him and licked her lips. "So, heading to the Big Apple alone? I notice you aren't wearing a wedding ring. Are you sure a good-looking guy like you will be safe in the big bad city all by your lonesome?"

John stood straight and took half-a-step back. What had this young woman just said? Suddenly, he got it. Embarrassment flooded through him. A flush crept into his cheeks. If he hadn't been so frantic and tangled up in his own thoughts, he might have noticed the signs. Or maybe not. It had been years since anyone had flirted with him. His heart plummeted in his chest. This would not end well.

Cara lifted her free hand and seductively twirled a lock of hair around a finger. "Do you have luggage?"

"Yep, just this one." He hoisted a little bag onto the scale.

Time was running out. Cara upped her game. "Looks like you're traveling light. Must not be staying too long. Maybe when you get back in town..." she stopped mid-sentence. No response. Not even a blink.

Cara sucked in a sharp, painful breath and rolled back her stiff shoulders.

She opened the ticket and began entering information onto the computer. "Okay, that's American Air Flight 1012, departing from gate C-12. Let me confirm your reservation." Fingers poised above the keyboard, she located his name. The young woman gasped. The few remnants of her saucy smile vanished altogether. Now mortified, Cara continued to input data, a tight professional smile nailed to her face. "Yes, you are confirmed through to New York. You can pick up your boarding pass at the gate."

John gave her an apologetic look. "Thanks a lot." He retrieved the ticket and left.

Cara stared after his retreating form and hissed out a disgusted breath. What a bust that had been. To think, Annie had taught her how to identify married men, lechers, even gay guys. But even worldly-wise Annie had never thought to tell Cara how to spot, of all things, a darn priest.

John strode through the terminal, navigating his way through clusters of passengers and tour groups that possessed far more luggage than sense. He passed through security, rode the escalator to the next level and made his way to gate C-12.

He thought about the ticket agent as he went. He regretted the interaction. How many times in recent years had he experienced similar situations? It was almost an occupational hazard. The moment people discovered he was a priest, everything changed. Some became cautious in their speech, others overly deferential. The worst of all were those who grew ridiculously pious as if they were on a first-name basis with God.

At the gate, John got his boarding pass and dropped into a molded plastic chair. The flight didn't take off for at least forty-five minutes. He smothered a groan. These days, spare time was no longer an asset, but a liability. It translated into yet another opportunity to think. And John had done enough thinking lately, enough for at least two or three lifetimes.

Unbidden, the nagging question popped back into his overwrought mind and ricocheted around and around. Had he made the right decision to go to New York?

He swallowed hard, trying to quell the escalating anxiety. He clenched and unclenched one fist on his lap. So many individuals would be impacted. Lives would be irrevocably altered. And what about his own future? He had been a priest for such a long time. And now? He gnawed on the various questions like a hungry dog with a meaty bone.

Too nervous to remain seated, John jumped up and wandered over to the bank of floor-to-ceiling windows. In the distance, a sleek airplane came into view. It slid through the sky, growing in mass as it approached the runway. Beams of sunlight glinted off the silver fuselage as the airplane angled toward the earth.

John edged closer to the glass, tracking its progress. The jet touched down, alighting on the tarmac as seamlessly as a butterfly on a flower petal. It glided along, without a care in the world. The priest smiled at the thought of an airplane having thoughts and emotions like human beings.

John's personal respite from worry was to be short-lived, for his mind seized on an issue even more troubling than his decision to go to New York. The murder threat. Was it real? Absolutely. There was no doubt about that.

A shudder of trepidation darted through him and the fine hair on the back of his neck bristled. As if in agreement, his heart stuttered in his chest at the thought of this profoundly troubling problem. God almighty, had he done the right thing in this situation? Or should he have told someone about it?

John hung his head and pressed his forehead onto the chilly glass, overwhelmed by the gravity of these recent decisions. He felt he had done the right thing in both cases. But could he be wrong?

II

LARRY CONSULTED HIS WATCH. Five minutes until the beginning of his shift. He clutched a cup of black coffee in one hand and scratched his corpulent belly with the other. Yawning, he considered the scores of people entering and exiting the airport. At once, he noticed the solitary figure positioned just inside the sliding glass doors, standing still as a stack of bricks. Beside him sat a black dog, a brown leather harness strapped to its back. Larry realized the man was blind and clearly needed assistance.

He clambered from the chair, hitched up the black trousers of his uniform and tossed the near-empty cup into a trash can.

Larry approached the pair. "Excuse me. I'm a security guard for the airport. Can I offer some help?"

The man turned his head in Larry's direction. "Yeah, I would really appreciate it. Getting around this place is pretty difficult for Samson with all this noise and activity."

"Let me tell you, it's hard for most people, no less a dog."

Larry sized up the man in an instant, an unconscious security guard habit. To label him as average would be an extreme over-statement. Completely forgettable was far closer to the mark. Everything about him was monochromatic: brown hair, clothes, and shoes. Not a single accessory, save the striking Labrador retriever with bright inquisitive eyes and dense glossy fur now standing alongside him. The dog swung his ebony head this way and that, obviously enthralled with the hustle and bustle of the airport.

What a shame, Larry thought to himself. If the clothes and dark glasses didn't give the guy's disability away, the dog sure as hell did.

The guard was intrigued by what the lab wore. He was draped with some sort of yellow-and-green plaid plastic affair. It covered his back and sides. He asked the man, "What's with these fancy duds on the dog?"

"It's a raincoat. The guide dog school gives them to us. They are predicting bad weather back East."

"Well, I'll be darned. You learn something new every day," Larry said. "So, know your gate number?"

"Yes. It's C-12."

"Okay. Come with me. I'll have you there in a jiff."

The man slung the flight bag over his shoulder and placed a hand on Larry's upper arm. The men negotiated the crowds in the terminal. The guard noticed the man's death grip on his arm. He hung back, fidgeted and shuffled uncomfortably as his shoulders brushed up against fellow travelers. Sweat from the man's palm seeped through Larry's light cotton shirt. His anxiety was nearly palpable.

At the security station, Larry took the flight bag and parked it in an empty bucket on the conveyer belt. "Got any change, keys? I'll need your shoes. Ever since 9-11 last year, passengers practically have to strip down to their underwear."

The man complied. "How about I go through the metal detector first," Larry suggested. "Then you and Sam follow along."

He paused. "Sure, I can follow you. But could someone take Sam around to the other side? The metal in his harness always triggers the alarm and it frightens him."

"No problem." Larry liberated the leash from the man's grip. "Come on, boy, now that's a good dog." He maneuvered the Lab in the cramped space, then handed the leash to the woman working behind the counter.

He returned to his charge. "Now, come with me."

But the disabled man didn't budge. "But Samson, where is he?"

Baffled, the guard darted a glance over at the man, wishing he could see past the mirrored lenses of the dark glasses.

The blind man now appeared far more than merely anxious—he was completely unhinged. His face was a study in pure panic. His breath was coming in rapid jerks. His right hand stretched out, ineffectually groping the empty air.

What the hell, Larry marveled. Did he feel lost or frightened when separated from the dog? Like his replacement vision had also been stolen from him?

"My colleague has him. He's fine." Larry clamped a hand over the man's wrist and hurried forward. The detector didn't emit a single bleat of protest as the twosome moved through.

"There we go," Larry announced as he got the leash and slapped it back into the man's hand. After reclaiming his possessions from the appropriate bucket, they moved on.

The twosome approached the escalator. A flicker of concern ignited in Larry's mind. Would this be a problem, too? Yet, it proved simple for the man to execute. He never missed a beat.

However, the Lab was a different story. The dog was instantly distraught, as though the moving stairs were something never encountered before. Samson balked and braced his outstretched forelegs in an attempt to impede progress. He was terrified. The loosely held leash eventually pulled taut and dragged the unwilling animal aboard. He scrabbled for traction as the stairs divided. His toenails couldn't connect with the slick surface.

Throughout the brief journey, the dog whined pitiably. People riding the opposing escalator glowered with disdain at the security guard. Many whispered to one another behind cupped hands. The two men stepped off with alacrity. The dog bounded forward, leaping onto the platform as if shot from a cannon.

Larry was astonished by the lab's bizarre behavior. "Jesus. I thought they trained service dogs to go everywhere their owner goes."

"Oh, well, yes, of course, they do. Sam just has some funny quirks."

The guard shrugged, nonplussed. "Yeah, I guess … whatever."

Larry quickened his pace. In record time, they were at the gate, all checked in.

"Thanks so much for your help," the man said. "One more thing. Before you go, do you think you could show me to the men's room?"

"Certainly. It's on my way. In fact, it's right here next to your gate."

The guard located the restroom entrance. He placed the blind man's right hand on the brick wall. "Just follow this wall down about ten feet or so, turn left and you'll be there."

Doug Sanders thanked the guard and strode into the men's room. Against all odds, it was vacant. He headed directly to the handicapped cubicle, squeezing Sampson in beside him. Doug pitched the flight bag on the floor and pressed his forehead and opened palms flat against the locked stall door. For several minutes, he drew in deep breaths of air and exhaled slowly.

"What a shit show," he said in a whisper. The decision to keep his eyes closed throughout the charade to ensure legitimacy had been a mistake. The vertigo. The panic. The fear. These unforeseen consequences had completely overtaken him at the security station.

Authenticity be damned! From now on, these eyes were staying open. Then there was the fiasco with the escalator. Naturally, Samson would be afraid of stairs moving, shifting and dividing under his paws. *That poor guy.*

Doug shed his jacket and hung it on the hook. The sweat-soaked shirt beneath reeked of nervous fear. The dark glasses went into a shirt pocket. He squatted and stroked the dog's head.

"You're a good boy, Sam. Now, lay down. "He patted the tile floor with an open palm. Samson obeyed and lifted a forepaw in anticipation. But a belly rub was not on the agenda. Instead, Doug reached for the object securely taped beneath the harness strap. Teeth gritted, he unwound the sturdy adhesive, careful not to tug Sam's fur. Only a couple of seconds and he had it.

Doug eased onto the toilet seat and stared at his cupped hands. They held the gun, the weapon he had just successfully moved through airport security. Good God, *he had done it*. He slid a finger along the surface of the Glock as a man might trace the line of a lover's breast. The fact that the plan had actually worked was stunning.

Thump. Thump. Thump. Feet in the hallway. A man entering the restroom.

Doug drew in a sharp breath and held it. Time condensed to that exact moment. In his mind's eye, Doug saw himself sitting on the edge of a toilet in the San Diego airport...holding an actual gun. And someone was just outside the stall door, not ten feet away. Eyes dilated, Doug stared at the door lock.

Splashing water. The paper towel dispenser whirred.

Doug resumed breathing, shallow, staccato breaths. Sweat drizzled down his spine.

Silence. What was the man doing? Sam's back legs were poking out from underneath the door. Did this unexpected visitor see them?

You're blind; you're allowed to have the dog. You're blind... The mantra repeated in Doug's mind. But the gun. There was no plausible explanation for that.

Something slammed onto the counter. A plastic comb?

Oh, for fuck's sake, was the guy primping?

John examined his unkempt reflection in the restroom mirror. Washing his face and combing his hair had done little to improve his appearance. Thank God the reunion wasn't until tomorrow. He inspected his clothing. After the alarm clock debacle, he had just grabbed what was available. The burgundy button-down shirt was off by one button. At least the jeans were clean and somewhat new. John rebuttoned the shirt, tucked it in and smoothed the fabric with both palms. One final flick of the comb through his hair and that was as good as it was going to get. The priest walked over to the trash receptacle and disposed of the paper towel.

Three steps and the sound of something hitting a garbage can. More footfalls, now retreating down the hall.

Doug whimpered in relief, then reproached himself in the suffocating cubicle. "Get over yourself. It's a friggin' public restroom. What did you think was going to happen?"

Doug collected himself. Once homeostasis had been restored, he stood and eased the Glock into the shoulder holster. Sampson jumped up. His wagging tail swished on the underside of the plastic, sounding like windshield wipers scraping on frosty glass.

Doug empathized with the lab for having to endure so much. He unhooked the harness, pulled it over Samson's head and removed the plastic shroud. After the harness was replaced, he stowed the tape and now superfluous raincoat in the flight bag and shrugged back into his jacket.

Still shaken from the close call, Doug surveyed the men's room and stepped out. Dark glasses back in place, Doug stumbled to recapture the essence of being blind, this time with eyes open to narrow slits. *You just gotta make it onto the plane. The rest will be fine.*

He drew in a deep breath and picked up the harness. The man and dog exited the men's room and returned to the terminal.

III

THE AIRPORT COFFEE SHOP WAS unusually tranquil. The breakfast rush had come and gone. Only a handful of customers milled around, swilling coffee, reading newspapers.

One employee counted money at the cash register, while another swept the floor.

A server, eager to go on break, took a corner too fast. She clipped the edge of a table where a single man sat. The table rocked. Hot tea quaked in a cup and splattered onto the man's left hand and the edge of one sleeve.

The man flinched and yanked his hand back.

"Oh my gosh, "the server said. "I am so sorry. Are you all right?"

Dr. Gordon Brooks grabbed several stiff white napkins from the dispenser and dabbed at the mess. "Yes, sure, I am fine," he mumbled.

The woman peered closer. He looked anything but fine. The man simply radiated misery. His skin was slack and sallow, His face gaunt. His suit, probably expensive, looked as though it might have been worn throughout the previous day and night. "Can I get you more tea? Something to eat?"

He shook his head. "No thanks. I will be on my way shortly."

The server turned, took a single step and paused. She felt the soft nudge in her chest. At that, she turned and walked back. Without a moment of hesitation, she slipped onto the padded bench across from the wretched man.

Startled, the patron's eyebrows shot up.

"You look like you are carrying the weight of the world," she commented.

He gave a curt chuckle. "I am. My life is falling apart."

"Personal or professional."

"Honestly...both."

"On a scale of one to ten, with ten being the absolute worst."

He finished his tea, laid the cup aside along with the soggy napkin. "Ten, across-the-board."

She blew out a breath. "Wow, that's rough. Tell me about it?"

Gordon paused, considered. He flicked a glance around the room. "Don't you have something you need to do?"

"I'm doing it right now."

He dragged a hand down his face. "Well, three years ago, I married a woman much younger than me. It was stupid. An incredible mistake on so many levels. You know what they say, no fool like an old fool."

She shrugged. "Wouldn't be the end of the world," she replied. "People make mistakes all the time. And the professional thing?"

Gordon figured, in for a penny.... He took in a deep breath and spoke in a low tone. "I have been charged with manslaughter. If convicted, I could go to prison for the rest of my life. I would never practice medicine again."

"You're a doctor," she stated.

"Neurosurgeon." He turned his open palms up on the Formica table in a placating gesture. "I didn't do it."

She never broke eye contact. "I wasn't even going to ask."

A silence descended between them. Behind the counter, plates clanked, knives and forks clattered against one another. "It's going to be all right," she finally murmured.

He swung his head from side to side. His shoulders slumped, then deflated altogether. "I don't know, I just don't know."

He gave her a smile of the most infinite misery. "You have such kind, gentle eyes," he commented. "You remind me of someone I used to know...and love."

She smiled at the compliment, even though she knew it was meant for someone else. This man still loved this unknown woman, it was more than evident.

The waitress stood. "I'll pray for you."

His throat constricted with emotion, tears rushed to his eyes. He blinked several times. "I'm not really big on God."

"Don't worry, he's big on you."

She touched his shoulder. A comforting sensation started at the base of Gordon's spine. It fluttered up the center of his back then settled in his heart. He felt peaceful, calm. The feeling was so novel, so welcome. Gordon wished he could wrap his arms around himself and hold the fragile feeling safe within, so it could never, ever leave him.

The woman pivoted and walked away. He watched as she headed for the restaurant's entrance. Gordon remained still for a matter of seconds, then also extricated himself from the booth.

How could he possibly thank this woman for her compassion and generosity? He dug into a pocket and drew out all of his money. He placed it on the table, knowing it was tawdry gratitude, indeed. Would she even get it? Probably not. He made a mental note to discover who she was on his return and find some way to thank her.

Ten minutes later, Gordon was at gate C-12. He canvassed the waiting area for an empty seat. He paused in his quest and redirected his gaze. The brown-haired man in the dark purple shirt looked so familiar. Gordon strained to make an identification. The name was right there, nibbling around the edges of his mind. But try as he might, he could not reel it in.

Gordon spotted a vacant seat on the opposite side of the lounge. He wove through scattered handbags and carry-ons. His foot caught on something unseen. He stumbled, almost fell to his knees. He regained his equilibrium and whirled around. Gordon had every intention of chastising the person who had so carelessly blocked the aisle. He locked eyes with an enormous black dog and immediately bit back the angry words. *Mother of God. He had kicked a Seeing Eye dog and was preparing to berate a blind person.* "Sorry," Gordon mumbled to the man or the dog, he didn't know which.

Moving away with haste, he went down an adjoining aisle and dropped into a seat.

The doctor raked a palm through his sparse, graying hair. It was thinning on top, bald at the crown. Gordon threw back his head and closed his eyes. Morning sun splashed onto his shoulders, providing unexpected warmth. He thought again about the woman in the coffee shop. If angels existed, she was surely one of them. "Thank you," he said in a whisper.

IV

BRAD CASHMAN SPED ALONG THE road at a rapid clip; his lean frame arced over the blue 21-speed bike. The wind whipped through his dark hair and caused his unzipped lightweight jacket to flap behind him like untethered wings. His cheeks were tinged pink by the cold. He blinked furiously as the chill air assaulted his unprotected eyes. Every few minutes, he lifted one hand to brush away tears.

The early morning was quiet, undisturbed by the usual El Cajon commuter traffic. The silence was punctuated only occasionally by the trill of a songbird or the pop-pop of gravel beneath his rubber tires.

He pedaled along the familiar streets, crossing intersections and executing turns. He traveled by memory. This route was as recognizable to him as his own face in the bathroom mirror. As a young boy, he'd routinely bike out to Gillespie Field to see his father fly. But during the past few months, he'd been riding out to Gillespie, not to stand on the sidelines and watch, but to sit in the cockpit and fly.

Now as he zipped along the street, Brad marveled—today was the day, his first solo flight. Although hunched over his bike, Brad's chest puffed out a little at the idea of it. Not quite nineteen years old, and he was ready to fly alone. Even Anthony hadn't soloed until he was twenty. At the thought of his older brother, Brad's happy expression melted into a look of hate. Anthony, his father's favorite. That rat bastard was always the first to do everything and do it all so damn well. Could Brad help it if he'd been born second?

With one last turn, Brad embarked on the final leg of his journey, pedaling a little faster now. He sped past a scrawny brown dog tethered to a flagpole dozing in a narrow patch of morning sunlight. Brad called a greeting. The old dog lifted its graying muzzle a few inches, gave a perfunctory woof, and seemed to offer him a slight smile. The dog thumped its ragged tail twice in the dust before resuming its nap. Brad took this as a good omen for what the day held in store.

Skidding slightly on the entrance's uneven surface, Brad wheeled into the Gillespie Field parking lot. He waved a greeting to Cal, who was stepping down from his beat-up gray Bronco, a white paper bag clutched in one hand.

"Hey, I brought coffee," the flight instructor shouted over the hood of his old truck. He held the bag aloft. "Thought we might sit and talk a little before you go up."

Brad, braking to a stop, swung his right leg over the end of the bike. "Great," he called back. He automatically yanked his black biking shorts down, which had ridden up his skinny legs during the ride.

The two ambled over to a nearby bench and sat. The sun caused their individual shadows to stretch out before them. Cal reached into the bag, fished out the coffee, then handed a cup to Brad. He pulled off his own plastic lid. "So, think you're ready?"

"Yep."

"Scared?"

Brad tracked the progress of a small plane as it gradually lifted into the air from a distant runway. He turned back to Cal and admitted with a shrug, "Maybe a little."

The instructor gave his head a quick affirmative shake, his longish gray hair flopped to one side with the terse nod. "Good, you should be. If you said you weren't, I don't know if I'd let you go up alone."

"After all my big talk, if I went home today without flying solo, my dad would have my butt for dinner."

For several long moments, Cal examined Brad's face with a surgeon's precision. He'd been worried about this kid for a long time, concerned about his motivation behind learning to fly. Did he really want it for himself, or was he simply trying to please and impress his father, the highly-decorated Vietnam fighter pilot?

Cal believed he knew the answer. That's what worried him.

Hunching over, surveying the distant horizon, the instructor brought the paper cup to his lips and took a generous swallow. "Brad? You sure you want to do this today?"

Surprised by the question, Brad sat straight up on the bench. His towering shadow now eclipsed Cal's diminished shape. "What? Are you kidding? Of course I want to, I have to, I—"

The instructor cut him off. "Son, you don't have to do anything."

"Are you shitting me? Of course I do. These lessons were a graduation gift from my father. And besides, I want to do this, I really do."

Cal could see the boy struggling to convince himself of his own earnestness. His heart swelled with compassion, thinking of the tremendous pressure that must constantly be placed on those young, narrow shoulders.

Brad jumped to his feet and began pacing around in small circles like a dog gone rabid. "What's up with you, Cal? You've flown with me. You told me I was one of your best students. Are you saying now that I'm not good enough?"

The older man's expression softened. "Hey, come on back over here and sit down." Brad hesitated, then returned to his seat. Cal clapped a hand on the back of the boy's neck and gave it a gentle shake, regretting he'd ever brought the subject up. "Of course, you're good enough. I just wanted to make sure you were ready."

Brad stared down at his shoes. "Well, I am."

Cal got to his feet and swigged the remainder of his black coffee. "Then, let's do it."

Captain Dave Washburn entered the airport terminal and went directly to the American Air Operations room, where various flight attendants lingered about. He crossed to a bank of computers to access the crew list, check the fuel load, verify the weather, and retrieve the flight plans for the New York trip. Then he hustled onto the Boeing 767, while First Officer Marty Louis descended to the tarmac to conduct an exterior inspection of the aircraft. Settled in the cockpit, the pilot studied the aircraft maintenance book for recent write-ups as well as deferred scheduled repairs. He checked the fuel load and tested the cockpit systems.

Marty climbed into the cramped space and plunked down into the adjoining seat. "She's looking good out there, how's everything in here?"

"Good to go. Hey, want to hear some great news?"

"Sure."

"Remember that new car I've always been talking about?"

Marty scratched the back of his neck. "Yeah, a BMW, wasn't it?"

"Right. Well, Amy and the girls gave me a brand new Beemer for my forty-fifth birthday."

Marty gave a long, low whistle. "No way. That wife of yours is really something special."

Dave handed the flight plans to Marty. "You got that right."

Marty grunted and eyed the voluminous computer printout. "You know, someday these damn things are going to get so long, we're going to have to lay them out on the wing just to read them."

A couple of pages drifted to the cockpit floor; they went unnoticed.

V

DOUG RELAXED IN THE PLASTIC chair, legs stretched out before him on the functional carpet. Samson snoozed beside him, occasionally twitching a paw or curling a lip in a dream-inspired snarl. From his vantage point behind the opaque lenses, the man observed the room, careful to shift only his eyes. The extreme agitation experienced earlier had abated. Now, he was enjoying himself, savoring this unique moment in time.

He had to fight a wide grin from erupting on his face. Who would have thought impersonating a blind person could be so interesting? Watching other people watch him was intriguing as hell. Invariably, each new traveler entering the lounge would

31

glance curiously at Sam, then up at him, then back down to the dog, any number of possible emotions, everything from pity to admiration registering on their faces.

By far, small children proved the most entertaining of all since they had not yet been thoroughly indoctrinated with proper etiquette. Often they would point and stare wide-eyed, even blurt out an outrageous comment or two. A mortified parent would invariably swat their hand or drag them off to some remote corner, probably to have a little chat about inappropriate behavior.

He considered his own role as a parent. Had he ever spoken to Alex about such matters as the treatment of disabled people? Probably not.

Doug turned his attention to the man, the man who would soon be dead, a lifeless body housed in the morgue. To his genuine surprise, two men, the priest and the doctor, were both on this flight. Sure, Doug had heard of coincidence, but what were the odds of all three of them booking the identical flight?

Doug let it go. He vastly preferred to revel in the thrill of the moment. His heart thumped in his chest as he stared at the man, smug in the knowledge that he was as unrecognizable to his prey as a hunter dressed in camouflage is to an unsuspecting deer.

"Mr. Sanders?" A soft female voice roamed around the periphery of Doug's consciousness. "We're seating all of our pre-board passengers now."

Startled by the soft touch of a hand on his arm, Doug jerked in the chair.

"Oh my, I'm sorry I frightened you," the gate agent said.

"No, really, that's okay. I was just lost in thought." Samson leaped onto all fours. Doug fumbled to snag the leash before the dog dragged it off his lap.

"Is this your carry-on next to the dog?"

"Yes." Doug rose and eased Sam to his side.

"Alright, I've got the bag. Would you like to take my arm?"

He gripped her elbow and the agent escorted him down the jetway. On the aircraft, she stopped at the first row in coach. "Here's your seat," the woman pointed out and placed his hand on the arm. "We put you in the bulkhead so the dog would have more room."

Doug was chagrined. He hoped to be located in the rear of the plane. He wanted to keep tabs on the man throughout the flight. "I appreciate your thoughtfulness concerning the dog. However..." he cast about for a reasonable excuse for why this location wouldn't do. "I would prefer to sit closer to the back if that's possible," he began, then hesitated, still at a loss. A second later, it came to him. "It's the restrooms. It's so much easier for me to get to them if I'm in the back of the plane. Going through first-class with the dog is always a problem."

The agent was quick to respond. "I understand. We'll just switch you with another passenger." Doug followed her down the aisle.

"How about right here? You're just a couple of rows from the rear of the plane."

"Excellent." The man lowered himself into the tan cushioned seat and encouraged Sam to lie down.

Task completed, the agent left the plane.

With the first-class curtain drawn aside, Doug discovered he could see all the way to the front of the plane. Within seconds the target was there, stepping onto the aircraft and advancing down the aisle. He kept walking, passing row after row. Eventually, he eased into a seat directly across the aisle from Doug.

This was unbelievable. Doug could observe the man throughout the flight as he spoke his last words, ate his final meal, never knowing he would soon be dead.

A young woman knelt next to Doug's seat and gave Sam's head a pat. "My name is Shelly. I am one of your flight attendants today. Is there anything I can help you with prior to take off?"

"Thanks, but I'm good."

"You look like a happy guy; meeting someone special in New York?"

Doug grinned. "You could say that."

The flight attendant gave his forearm a squeeze. "Good for you. I will be back to get drink orders for both you and your pup as soon as we are in the air." She rose and returned to the rear of the plane.

VI

SABRINA WALSH STOOD POISED IN the open cabin doorway with the requisite flight-attendant smile plastered on her face. She welcomed yet another passenger onto the plane. "If we get any more, we're going to have to start stuffing them in the overhead bins," she commented through clenched teeth to the perky young woman positioned alongside her. She then called "hello" for perhaps the one-hundredth time that morning.

"No kidding," Meredith Rowan agreed, her voice lowered to a stage whisper. "Why the heck does everyone want to go to New York, anyway?"

Sabrina fluffed several strands of curly auburn hair away from her eyes. "Got me, especially now with all that bad weather. And why are they all on our flight?"

"Just lucky, I guess." Meredith shrugged, then announced in an elaborately casual voice, "New York, personally, I think that city is just abysmal."

Sabrina dropped her fists onto both hips. "Abysmal? Did you really just say that?"

An impish smile crept across Meredith's face. "Great word, isn't it? And I sprung it on you before we even got in the air. I deserve extra points for that one."

"I can't take it anymore." Sabrina slapped her forehead with an open palm. "That word-a-day calendar of yours will be the death of me."

Straightening to her full height, Meredith adopted a superior look. "Hey, there's nothing wrong with self-improvement. You watch, it will pay off someday."

"Right. When I absolutely refuse to fly with you anymore, you can mention how abysmal it is to lose your best friend."

"Oh, you're not fooling me. You're just jealous because the bookstore only had one calendar left, on sale no less. And I got it." Meredith flicked a quick glance down the aisle. "Looks like there's some confusion about seating in the back, guess I'll go and help. You okay up here?"

"Sure, no problem. It looks as if we just have a few more stragglers coming on. I'll get them taken care of, then check out with Ken."

"Okay, I'm off. Wish me luck. If you hear screaming, send reinforcements."

"Roger that," she called as Meredith swept down the aisle. Sabrina returned to the door and greeted the few final travelers as they boarded the plane.

"That all of them?" the attendant asked the gate agent standing a few feet away from her on the jetway, clipboard and ballpoint pen in hand.

Ken jotted some final notations. "We have one first-class who might still make it. We were instructed to hold as long as possible. But, as of right now, that's it. So, want me to round up a few more standbys and send them your way?"

"Just to keep my life interesting?"

"You could double up. Now tell me, could it get any better than this?" he parried as he flipped a few sheets over the clipboard, then shoved the pen into his shirt pocket.

"I sure hope so," Sabrina replied as she retreated into the plane.

VII

GORDON FASTENED HIS SEATBELT AND placed his leather briefcase on his lap. He extracted the speech he would give tomorrow at the medical conference. Additional leg room would have been greatly appreciated in the cramped space. Unfortunately, by the time the authorities gave him the green light to attend the conference in New York, first class was sold out.

The doctor began reading. Within seconds, a look of profound bewilderment spread across his face. The words seemed only vaguely familiar, even though he had written this speech less than one week ago. Now, it seemed as strange to him as a conversation spoken in a foreign language.

He lowered the papers to his lap and contemplated the future. Gordon knew he had the best legal team that money could buy, but was that enough? The evidence against him was more than damning.

Panic streaked through the doctor. His continued existence as a free man depended on a handful of lawyers proving his innocence, convincing the world that he was not guilty of taking a life, killing that old man. Prison. It was an unthinkable concept. He looked out the little window, then back at the speech. He must concentrate. Eyebrows pinched together, he squinted at the paper. Yet, fatigue remained the victor. The black type leaped about the page like hailstones striking cement. Gordon capitulated, loosened his tie, then sat back and waited for the plane to take off.

"How about playing Gameboy with me?"

John regarded the little boy in the adjoining seat. "Not right now." He gestured to the magazine. "See, I'm right in the middle of this article and—"

"When will you be done?" the kid blurted out. He popped up in his seat and perched on the cushioned edge.

The priest was rapidly growing weary of this child. His name was Jeffery and already he had asked John to read him a story, color with him and take him to the restroom.

The boy persisted. "So how long?"

"How long what?"

Jeffery gazed bug-eyed through his thick glasses. In a slow, distinct voice, he reiterated, "How long until you're done with the article?"

John affected the same tone. "I don't know, I haven't read it yet."

Piqued by not getting his own way, the child screwed up his face and stuck out his lower lip. "But mom said I'd have someone to play with on the plane."

"Where's your mother, anyway?"

"My mom and dad are divorced. She stays here while I visit him in Buffalo. She's in the airport right now, waiting for me to take off."

John's heart softened. "Listen, let me finish this article and then we'll do whatever you want."

The youth bounced up and down in his seat. "Really?"

"Sure...promise."

Satisfied, Jeffery went back to his electronic game. John returned to the article. He scanned paragraph after paragraph, but was unable to locate his place. He flipped back to the table of contents.

"Great, you're finally done." The kid bent down and whipped out his coloring book from the flight bag on the floor. "Now we can color together!"

Resigned, John dropped the tray-table. He selected a crayon and set to the task of bringing color and life to Barney the Dinosaur.

VIII

SABRINA CONSULTED HER WATCH, then peaked down the jetway. Empty. Briefly, she wondered if this final first-class passenger would make the flight. "Better get the lead out if you want to go to New York this morning," she muttered under her breath to this unknown person.

Turning, she released the microphone from its wall mounting and raised it to her lips. She cleared her throat and announced, "Good morning and welcome to American Air flight 1012 to New York City. Our traveling time today will be approximately..."

One of the flight attendants was speaking on the public address system. Doug endeavored to hear over the din of passengers conversing with one another, shoving bags in overhead compartments and snapping out instructions to small children. He caught a word or two here and there. It was just the standard airline greeting.

Doug stole a surreptitious look at the man across the aisle, thrilled anew by his own anonymity. Just a little over six hours and the target would be dead.

The strategy was perfect, refined to include the minutest details. Recently, Doug had taken the identical American Air flight, traveling as a sighted person. With great precision he had executed the plan. He evaluated the exact amount of time it would take to slip into the men's room, relieve Sam of the bogus harness, change his own clothes, return to the terminal as a non-disabled man with a pet, then escort Sam to the ticket counter where he would be crated-up for the return flight home. The timing was flawless.

Doug would then descend to baggage claim, where his victim would be waiting amidst scores of other passengers. All eyes would be glued to the rotating carousel. He would simply edge up behind the man, shoot him two or three times in the back, then fade away, melting into the throng.

The silencer would ensure the shots would go undetected. When the man fell to the floor, a degree of confusion, perhaps even mild hysteria, would surely catapult through the crowd. Once the blood and wounds were noticed, everything would turn on a dime.

Knowing a killer was loose in the crowd, the group mindset would instantaneously shift from shock to fear. Instead of drawing nearer to lend assistance, people would recoil and retreat from the crumpled body. Pandemonium would ensue. By the time order had been restored, Doug would be seated comfortably at an American Air gate. He would be in another set of clothes with the brown dye washed from his hair, patiently waiting for the return flight to San Diego.

Now, sitting sedately in his seat, Doug allowed his eyes to slide shut. His rambling thoughts played out from this day forward, unraveling into the future. Tonight, he would return home. Tomorrow, he would begin a new life.

The man's death would be an exorcism, setting Doug free from the malignant cancer that had grown inside him for so long. Finally, the slate would be wiped clean. Doug would have peace and happiness once more...yes, peace and happiness once more.

Gradually, Doug's head lolled to one side. Behind the dark glasses and closed eyes, his overwrought mind tumbled into a state of infinite relaxation. His thoughts drifted along of their own accord, unhampered by the logical constraints of the conscious mind. As if sitting in a movie theater, Doug watched the life he longed for so desperately, unfold. It dissolved from scene to scene with great rapidity.

He was living in his Coronado condominium. Samson was scampering around on the grass playing with his tennis ball.

And Pam was back, enveloped in his arms, loving him as she once had. Best of all, Alex was there. The three of them were a happy family, again. They would stay that way forever and ever and ever.

At once, the mental motion picture ended, the final scene a freeze-frame of the three of them with huge grins etched into their faces.

Doug fell into a deep sleep. The lines of tension and sorrow chiseled into his face disappeared, replaced by a faint, yet definitely discernible smile.

IX

SABRINA COMPLETED THE ANNOUNCEMENT WELCOMING the passengers. In the next second, she heard the sound of pounding feet running along the jetway. She turned toward the open door. Ken completed his final few strides, change jingling noisily in his pocket, rubber-soled shoes squeaking, clipboard papers flapping about crazily. He executed a quick stop on the threshold of the plane.

Sabrina stepped forward. "What's the matter?" she asked in alarm.

Panting, Ken combed his hair back with one hand. "Don't close this door." He whacked the back of his clipboard against

47

the cabin door as if she might not know what door he was talking about.

"Why?"

"Remember that final passenger, the one I told you about in first-class?"

"Uh-huh."

"Well, she's here. Saw her myself, checking in. She'll be here in a sec."

"Who is she?"

"You won't believe it." Ken ignored the question, now straightening his striped tie and fastidiously brushing a speck of lint from the lapel of his dark suit.

"Ken, who is it?" she pressed, becoming more than a bit frustrated with him.

He gave her a dumb-mutt grin. "I want you to be surprised. Like I was. You're just not going to believe it." He whirled around and retraced his steps of moments earlier. He now strode along in a controlled, dignified manner.

Sabrina heaved a sigh of bafflement mixed with a fair share of annoyance. She stepped back to the wall and pulled the microphone from its hook. She didn't know what the heck was going on, but one thing she did know for certain was Meredith would skin her alive if she wasn't in on it. Sabrina spoke into the mike. "Will passenger L. Meredith please ring your call button, passenger L. Meredith?"

She saw her friend emerge from the rear galley and zip up the aisle. "What's up?" Meredith asked as she closed the gap between herself and Sabrina.

She shrugged. "I really can't say. All I know is we are expecting someone in first-class who, at least according to Ken, is pretty spectacular."

Meredith barged past Sabrina, craned her neck and darted a swift glance around the open cabin door. She lurched back as if yanked by an invisible hook. "Spectacular? No shit."

"Who is it," Sabrina pushed past her friend and peeked down the jetway. "Oh my gosh," she uttered in amazement. Then, she commanded out of the corner of her mouth, "Get over here beside me, and for once in your life, try to act professional."

Meredith sidled up next to her. The two women watched as the most strikingly gorgeous woman either one of them had ever seen sauntered down the series of ramps, flanked by Ken and another agent. She wore a sleeveless peach blouse with matching silk pants and a hat festooned with flowing peach ribbons that cascaded down her back. She laughed with the men as she walked. Her head threw back gaily as she smiled. It was the same smile all had seen dozens of times before on magazine covers, billboards and countless television commercials.

The entourage drew near. Ken edged forward and announced, "Sabrina and Meredith, I'd like you to meet—"

But they cut him off before he had the chance to complete the introduction. "Shea," they said in unison as the model boarded the plane.

Sabrina availed herself of the unique opportunity to scrutinize the celebrity up close. Tall, slender, with abundant brownish-blonde hair that fell about her shoulders in soft waves. Flawless, luminescent skin that seemed to radiate outward, as if an interior light glowed from within. Enormous eyes of the most spellbinding green that a casual observer would swear a color so unique and vibrant could only be the result of tinted contact lenses. She had a dimple, no less, at one corner of her perfect mouth.

As with so many of those in the public eye, Sabrina had always wondered if Shea Lansing was truly that exquisite. Or, did she just photograph well. Now she knew. Shea, perhaps the highest paid model in the world, was unquestionably one of the most extraordinarily beautiful women God ever created.

"I never thought it was possible, but you are even more stunning in person," Meredith breathed with great animation.

"Thank you. It's so kind of you to say that," Shea responded graciously. "I'm so sorry I'm late. The traffic was so much worse than we had anticipated. I hope I haven't held you up."

Meredith rushed to reassure her. "No, of course not. Look! We're still here on the tarmac." She hitched her chin toward the windows and the runway beyond. "We haven't even taken off yet."

Sabrina cringed, horrified. She wanted to gouge her friend in the ribs with an elbow, but knew it wouldn't go unnoticed by the others. Instead, she settled for giving Meredith a withering look, intended to get her to shut up. Of course, it didn't work at all.

Meredith blushed crimson. "Oh my God. I can't believe I said that. *Of course we haven't taken off yet.* What a stupid thing to say."

Shea reached out and clasped a beautifully manicured hand around Meredith's wrist. A constellation of gold bangles tinkled like wind chimes along her bare forearm. "Hey, no big deal, don't worry about it. Now, do you have a seat somewhere for me, or will I have to sit on the captain's lap?"

Meredith giggled. "Boy, wouldn't he love that."

Sabrina, unwilling to chance another blunder, stepped forward. "Your seat is right here." She gestured toward first-class with one hand. "Just let me show you."

"Great. Thank you." Shea followed the attendant. She was seemingly unaware of the dozens of curious eyes trained on her as she was ushered to her seat.

"What are you looking at?" Jeffery asked.

John, who had been gazing down the empty aisle toward the front cabin, turned back to the boy. "Oh, I just recognized someone. The woman who just got on the plane is a friend of mine."

"Do I know her?"

John chuckled. "No, I doubt that. But I bet your mom does."

Incredulous, Jeffery asked, "Why would you say that? You don't even know my mother."

"True. But this woman is a big celebrity, someone very well known."

"She's like, famous? Is she in the movies?"

"No, but she's on television and in lots of magazines."

"Really, TV? Can I meet her?"

John considered the request. "Sure, why not. Once we are airborne, you and I can go up to first class. Her name is Shea. She's very pretty and very nice."

"We haven't even taken off yet?" Sabrina hissed at Meredith in a mocking, singsong voice once she returned to the first-class galley. "Are you kidding me?"

"Holy crap, I still can't believe I said that." Meredith slapped both hands over her eyes.

"Well, I sure can." Sabrina was more than prepared to launch into a gratifying diatribe about choosing one's words more carefully. Yet, as the absurd scene replayed in her mind, all thoughts of rebuke vanished. She dropped her forehead against the padded wall and dissolved into a torrent of laughter. It was infectious. Soon, tears were streaming down both of their faces.

"Oh God, I'm going to wet my pants." Meredith doubled over, pressing her knees together.

Sabrina knew this was altogether possible because she'd seen it happen before. She laughed all the harder. Only after taking in several deep breaths to calm themselves were they able to regain some semblance of control.

"Sabrina?"

"Yeah," Sabrina rummaged in her purse, retrieved a compact, then set to repairing her tear-streaked makeup.

"Will you do me a favor?"

"Probably. What is it?"

"Can I switch places with you for this one flight?"

Sabrina looked up from the compact mirror. "You want to work first-class?"

"Yeah, I know you bid for it and all, but, but..."

"You just want to be around Shea," Sabrina finished.

"Yeah, I really do. Maybe we could talk a little and I could learn something from her. You know how I've always thought about doing some modeling on the side. Maybe she could give me a few tips. We could just tell Dave I'm working number one this shift. What do you say?"

"Well..."

"Come on," Meredith coaxed. "Just this one flight. It's really important to me."

Sabrina lifted an eyebrow. "Important enough to throw out that calendar?"

Meredith looked stricken. "My word-a-day? You'd actually make me get rid of it?"

"Uh-huh. After all, I want to get something out of this deal, too. It's not as if I relish working coach. Last time I checked, serving twenty-one passengers is a heck of a lot easier than nearly two-hundred." She gave her forehead one last swipe with the powder puff before flipping the compact closed and tossing it back into her purse.

Meredith lifted her chin, resigned. "Okay, if that's what it takes, I'll do it."

"Then first class is yours, and I'm out of here." Sabrina stowed her purse in the assigned bin, then stepped out into the aisle. "Have fun." She strode away, chuckling to herself as she passed row after row of passengers. Did Meredith really think that Sabrina would make her throw away her beloved calendar? Not in a million years. If Meredith wanted to try out new words on her for the next decade, it was fine with her.

Sabrina slid into her seat alongside the other attendants at the rear of the plane. She made a mental note to tell Meredith the minute they landed that she could keep the calendar.

X

BRAD CASHMAN CLIMBED INTO THE Cessna 150, slammed the door behind him and secured his seatbelt. He sat still and gazed around the interior of the small plane. He was all alone. A small shudder, half excitement, half trepidation, shot through him.

Cal stood on the edge of the tarmac, hands shoved into his baggy pants pockets. An expectant look was stamped on his face.

Brad flashed the instructor a thumbs up gesture through the cockpit window and Cal responded in turn.

Brad licked his dry lips. *Okay now, think. You know what you are doing." Verify fuel load, check. Review the flight instruments, check. Don't throw up or crap your pants, check. Start the engine.* And with a flick of the ignition, power began to pulse through the small aircraft.

He called the tower to receive clearance, then taxied to the designated position for departure. Waiting, he sucked in his lower lip. A deep furrow creased his normally smooth forehead. He gazed around the cockpit. Was that it? Wasn't there one more thing? It niggled at him like an unscratched itch.

Brad pivoted in his seat. Cal still stood poised at the edge of the tarmac. He desperately wanted to go back and run it by him. Cal would have the answer. But he couldn't do it. Anthony would never have to ask for help. A slight wave of nausea washed over him. He tamped it down, then just waited for the tower to give him the go-ahead. *Come on, it can't be that big of a deal, or I would have remembered.*

Within inches of Brad's hand was the black transponder box. It housed the device by which air traffic control and other planes would see the Cessna on their respective radar and Terminal Collision Avoidance System. The transponder remained switched off.

Brad received clearance from the tower; his attention was immediately riveted to the instrument panel. All lingering concerns were relegated to the back of his mind. Eyes pinned on the runway stretching out before him, left hand gripping the yoke, right hand wrapped securely around the throttle, Brad executed a perfect takeoff.

Holy shit. I did it. A textbook take off. Dad should have seen it. He headed in a westerly direction and allowed himself to take a much-needed breath. He laughed a little in self-congratulations.

Brad reviewed his flight plans. He would vector south, fly along the border for a few minutes, then return to Gillespie Field. He loosened his death-grip on the yoke and grinned with confidence as he eased the Cessna into a southerly heading.

"And in the unlikely event of a water landing, your seat cushion can also be used as a floatation device," Meredith explained over the PA. Three attendants, one in first-class, two in coach, demonstrated the versatility of the seat cushion.

Shea sat in her spacious seat with an economics textbook propped in one hand and a yellow felt-tipped marker poised in the other. Absently, she gnawed her lip in concentration as she studied the book, occasionally highlighting a specific passage. She had removed her hat and gathered her abundant hair to one side. Now, it spilled over one shoulder like a waterfall, casting half her face in shadow.

Gordon stared drowsily out the window. He grew mesmerized by the blur of scenery as the airplane taxied down the runway. Lulled by the hum of the engines, his eyelids fluttered once, twice, then fell closed.

The priest returned his tray-table to the upright position. Jeffery closed the coloring book and dropped the crayons into his flight bag.

"Can we color again when the plane takes off?" the boy requested hopefully.

"Absolutely," John confirmed. "After all, we can't leave poor Barney half-colored now, can we? That just wouldn't be right. I think he is really counting on you and me to come through for him."

"I think so, too!" Jeffery giggled. His eyes sparkled behind the coke-bottle glasses. He turned away to look out the window.

Sabrina couldn't stand it anymore. That darn restroom door was going to drive her to distraction. Every time she flew this particular aircraft, that door, with its constant shaking and rattling, got on her nerves. No matter how many times a maintenance request was filed, nothing ever got done. Well, she'd show that stinking door. It couldn't get the better of her.

Unclipping her seatbelt, she jumped to her feet and stalked over to the offender. Grabbing the knob, she twisted hard, yanked it open, slammed it shut. There, the rattling stopped.

Sabrina strode back to her seat, buoyed-up with self-righteousness, as if she'd just scored a major victory over the evils of shoddy workmanship. If she had been a gunslinger in the Old West, by God, she would have paused to blow the lingering wisps of gray smoke from the tip of her six-shooter. Instead, she merely contented herself with the appreciative glances and approving nods afforded her by the other attendants.

The sound of the slamming door ripped through the rear cabin. Doug sprang up in his seat. Perplexed, disoriented, cobwebs of sleep still cloaking his mind, he glanced about, uncertain of his surroundings. In a rush, it all came back.

His heart pounded against the walls of his chest. He counted to ten, then cautiously surveyed the area. No one had noticed him. Most of his fellow travelers appeared to be engrossed with the changing landscape outside their windows. Relieved, Doug unfurled the fingers of his clenched fists and relaxed back into the seat.

XI

FIRST-OFFICER MARTY LOUIS SCRUTINIZED the checklist one final time. "That about does it. The takeoff checklist is complete, Captain."

Dave eased the throttle back to decrease power and brought the aircraft to a standstill just short of runway 27. "Good, it looked complete to me, too. I'm going to signal the crew. You go ahead and notify the tower that we're ready."

Dave pushed a button on the overhead instrument panel. A chime sounded throughout the cabin; the attendants eased into their seats and fastened their belts.

Marty depressed a button on his yoke, then spoke. "American Air 1012 Heavy ready for take off."

Within moments, a clipped response returned from the tower, advising them to take position and hold on runway 27.

Dave maneuvered the jet to the designated location and reduced power once again. More than eight-thousand feet of open runway stretched out before him. Drumming his fingertips on the yoke, he scanned the horizon as he waited for clearance. It was a brilliant sun-drenched morning. The robins-egg blue sky remained unmarred by a single cloud. A light breeze wafted in from the West. It was excellent flying weather.

Brisk instructions from the tower cut through Dave's musings. They were clear to go. Dave slowly eased the throttle forward, increasing power. Soon, the thunderous whine of the two massive engines reverberated through the cockpit as the 767 sped down the runway.

Dave pulled back the yoke and the jet eased off the ground. The moment the plane became airborne, a familiar rush shivered through the pilot. Regardless of how many years he had flown, the actual conversion from ground to air still thrilled him. It was as if an enormous hand cupped beneath the belly of the aircraft was lifting the plane aloft, allowing it to become one with the sky.

The jet took off on a westerly heading, the Pacific Ocean shadowed darkly beneath its massive wings. Dave maintained a minimum climb speed. As they rose higher, he accelerated automatically. Once sufficient altitude had been achieved, Dave retracted the flaps and slats.

At five miles out, the tower told him to switch over to departure control and new orders were conveyed to turn left to a heading of 140 degrees and climb to eight-thousand feet. The pilot realigned the plane slightly to the East toward Tijuana. They would proceed eastwardly along the border a short distance before redirecting farther left toward New York.

Unexpectedly, the relative peace and quiet of the cockpit was fractured. A loud bell shrilled. A computerized voice declared, "Fire, right engine." Seconds later, the right engine fire handle on the console lit up.

Although startled, Dave's reaction was instantaneous, the product of trained reflex. He silenced the bell, eased the right throttle back and turned off the right fuel control switch. He grabbed the lighted handle and pulled. This isolated the problem engine by shutting off all fuel, bleed-air and hydraulics to it.

"God almighty," he murmured under his breath. He placed his hand on the good throttle and added additional power to compensate for loss of thrust. Dave and Marty exchanged an anxious glance.

Dave gripped the yoke and drew in a long breath. "Okay, discharge the first fire bottle, right engine. Then get Departure Control and tell them what's going on. Inform them that we're returning immediately."

As Dave issued orders, Marty grabbed the manual, locating the necessary checklist for this specific emergency. "How much fuel?" he requested. He extended a hand, grasped the lighted handle and turned it decisively to the right. This discharged a fire bottle in the right engine, containing a chemical designed to extinguish a fire on contact. He released the handle and hit the elapsed-time clock.

"Sixty-thousand pounds," Dave called out a fraction of a second before Marty spoke to Departure Control.

"American Air 1012 Heavy, we are declaring an emergency," the first officer explained. "We have a fire in our right engine and are carrying sixty-thousand pounds of fuel. Our intention is to return to Lindbergh field. We request the ILS runway 27 with crash trucks standing by. We'll keep you advised."

As confirmation was received from Departure Control, the elapsed-time clock completed its thirty-second rotation. The fire handle remained illuminated. The fire still burned.

"Come on, you bitch." Marty grasped the handle a second time. On Dave's command, he jerked it to the left. The second, and only remaining fire bottle, was discharged.

Marty slapped the clock again and returned to his checklist. The seconds ticked away.

Jaw clenched in determination, Dave focused all his attention on flying the plane. He was keenly aware of the clock. It approached the thirty-second mark. Together, he and Marty stared at the console. The time ran out. The handle, like an evil talisman, continued to glow.

"Well, shit. Those fire bottles really came through. Reminds me of some of the women I've dated lately." The tremor in Marty's deep voice belied the sarcasm of his words.

Dave scowled. "Yep. This is bad." Both fire bottles gone and the engine still burned. "But, come on. How many times have we worked through engine fires in the simulators? This is what we train for. This bird can still fly and the airport is only minutes away. You know we can do this."

Dave gave his friend the most positive look that he could muster. "Hey, now I can show you my new car. You call approach control and apprise them of the situation. I'll brief the attendants."

Dave grabbed a handset and punched the button four times. It signaled an emergency interphone call. Although the successive chimes could be heard throughout the cabin, only seven people realized an emergency was at hand. Each woman discontinued her current task and picked up the nearest phone.

Dave spoke, his words brisk. "We have a fire in the right engine. We are returning to the airport immediately. We don't anticipate an evacuation. If that changes, I'll use Easy Victor three times over the PA. We should be on the ground in six minutes. Crash trucks will meet us. Prepare the cabin."

The attendants, galvanized by the captain's words, swarmed into their respective cabins. They checked to make sure seatbelts were fastened, tray-tables and seats were up and locked and carry-on luggage remained stowed.

Rattled, Meredith stepped forward to address the passengers. She raised the hand mike to her lips, then hesitated. She tried to settle her nerves before speaking. The captain's announcement had come as no surprise. From her position at the front of the plane, she had heard the fire bell go off some time ago.

Meredith had been holding her breath in anticipation since that moment. She had never experienced an engine fire before, but knew, thankfully, that it would be contained. What's more, Captain Dave was a seasoned pilot with years of experience under his belt. She was scared, not terrified, but definitely concerned. How she wished Sabrina was here beside her right now to tease her out of her fear. Perhaps she'd sneak back and talk to her once everything was under control. But now, she had to make that damn announcement.

Meredith hooked her hair behind one ear, fiddled with her dangling earring, and sought the appropriate words. She swallowed hard, her mouth dry as dust. "Ladies and gentlemen, the captain has informed us there is a problem with one of our engines. This necessitates a return to the San Diego airport. At this point, we ask you to please remain in your seats."

Throughout the plane, passenger reaction to Meredith's words was fairly predictable. Most grumbled with irritation, while others digested the news in a more silent, stoic fashion. Inexplicably, a few travelers, either dismayed over their trip to New York, or delighted to return to California, actually whooped boisterously.

Shea scrutinized Meredith's face. She thought the attendant appeared a little pale. A small flicker of concern seemed to be playing around the corners of her mouth. Was she telling the truth about the nature of the problem or was it more severe? It troubled Shea somewhat, but the thought of possibly talking to her boyfriend again in San Diego, negated all lingering concerns. She placed her handbag under the seat and then checked to ensure her seat belt was secure. She settled back and waited to land.

"We're going back?" Jeffery asked.

"Looks like it." John, distracted, was consumed with his own thoughts about the aborted flight.

The little boy's expression grew worried and scared. "But, what am I going to do? Mom's probably already left for home. How will I find another plane? Who will—?"

John, responding to the fear suffusing the boy's face and words, placed his big hand on top of the little one gripping the armrest and patted reassuringly. He cut right in on the list of concerns. "Don't worry. I'll take care of you."

Jeffery, lips still trembling, asked, "You will?"

"Of course I will. After all, we're friends, aren't we?"

The kid's voice faltered, unsure. "Yes?"

"And friends take care of each other, right?"

He nodded his head, concern draining from his little face. "Right."

John reached over and tousled Jeffery's hair. "Then you have absolutely nothing to worry about."

The concern vanished as quickly as it had materialized. "Can I still meet the lady?"

"Lady?"

"The pretty one; the one my mom knows."

John finally caught on. "Oh, you mean Shea."

The boy nodded enthusiastically.

"You bet," the priest said. "We will catch up with her in the airport or on our next airplane."

"Son of a bitch," Doug swore aloud when he heard the announcement. He wanted to scream in frustration. He had to concentrate, devise a new strategy. But his rage was so profound it eclipsed all rationality. He dropped his head onto the seat back, breathing deeply, trying to regain a degree of control. Time. He just needed time to devise a new plan.

XII

DAVE CHECKED HIS INSTRUMENT PANEL again. He implemented the most recent instructions from approach control. The right engine was gone, but the fire was isolated. He knew the jet could execute the left turns required to return to Lindbergh Field. He began the descent to four-thousand feet while slowly turning left onto a northerly heading. Marty continued to review the emergency procedure for engine-fire shutdown and examine the checklist for an overweight landing.

At forty-five hundred feet, just under two miles from the American Air jet, Brad relaxed in the cockpit of the Cessna 150. Per his visual flight plans, he redirected the aircraft onto a westerly heading. He tilted his head to the left and could see

Tijuana just ahead. He thought he might take her up a few hundred feet, just for a little additional practice. Still glancing out the left window at the rocky landscape below, Brad pulled back on the yoke and began his ascent.

Dave completed the left turn descent. Marty extended a hand toward the instrument panel and caught a glimpse of something out of the corner of his eye. A plane? *A small airplane? It wasn't possible. It just wasn't...*

The visual impression never had time to fully register on the first-officer's mind, just as Brad Cashman never entertained another living thought. At just over forty-five hundred feet, the Cessna collided with the 767, ramming nose-first into the right wing, sheering off a portion of the side and back.

Like a bug flying into an electric fan, the small aircraft was instantly pulverized. Fragments of the wing, shards of the engine, and splintered segments of the fuselage careened into space, eventually drifting to the earth below.

The 767 quaked violently on impact. It pulled out of the left turn and continued on a level heading for the briefest of moments, as if independently considering its own course of action.

Dave blinked in horrified disbelief. "What the hell?" His elevated voice was punctuated by shock. Had the engine blown? He darted a questioning glance over at Marty.

The two men locked eyes. Fear sat suspended between them like an electric current. "Another airplane. It was another plane," the first officer croaked. His face reflected Dave's own expression of stark terror.

"No. It isn't possible. The TCAS. We didn't hear a thing."

A loud murmur rose in the cabin in the aftermath of the initial shudder. Travelers exchanged worried glances, some cried out in alarm. Others frantically pounded their flight attendant call buttons.

In the forward and aft galleys, the attendants were inundated with a symphony of chiming signals. Yet, no one stood to respond. They realized the plane was in serious trouble. And, though they didn't know what the problem was, they did know there was absolutely nothing they could do. So, helpless and scared, the women remained seated. They held each other's hands and waited.

The crippled wing dipped down. The jet began drifting to the right. Sweat poured down Dave's face and dripped onto his uniform. He panted through his open mouth like a fear-crazed animal. The captain struggled to fly the plane. He pounded maniacally on the controls. But, though the rudder remained intact and functional, the leading edge slats and ailerons on the right wing had been destroyed, along with the outer one-third of the wing itself.

His efforts rendered nothing; the plane defiantly continued its roll.

Marty slumped in his seat, staring into space. His eyes were glazed over as though he now existed in a catatonic stupor. One hand drooped at his side. The useless manual lay upside-down on the floor of the cockpit.

The aircraft tilted sideways. Terrified screams ripped through the cabin. Children wailed. Frightened adults clapped hands over their own mouths. Those occupying aisle seats on the left side of the plane were flung radically to the right. They bent awkwardly at the waist over the armrests like broken dolls. Here and there overhead bins opened, flinging carry-on items out like nickel candy spewing from a machine. Luggage rained down from above, striking passengers on their heads and shoulders. They shrieked in pain.

The jet dropped its nose and continued to roll to the right. It stopped at 50 degrees angle of bank, descending at a speed of two-thousand feet per minute. Mount Miguel came into view through the cockpit window. A scream of atavistic fear tore from Dave's throat.

"Help me. Dear Lord God, please help me," he implored the useless control panel. Tears zigzagged down his face. The mountain loomed closer and closer.

He yanked his sweat-drenched hands from the yoke, and clamped his arms over the top of his head as if this simple move could offer some sort of protection. A final thought of Amy and his two daughters flashed through his consciousness. Then it was gone.

The right wing and the nose of the aircraft struck first, taking the full impact of the mountain. The wing sheered off as the back of the aircraft swung around in a wide arch. It resembled the lashing tail of a massive Tyrannosaurus Rex. The remaining wing snapped in two. The plane split directly behind the left wing. As the jet twisted around the side of the mountain, the tail ripped free and was flung away, spinning off wildly.

The fuselage of the plane lodged in the side of the mountain at the three-thousand foot mark. It exploded into flames and launched a fireball skyward that could be seen for miles.

Search and rescue teams were dispatched to the site immediately. Dozens of paramedics from local hospitals followed. The ambulances couldn't manage the rough mountain terrain, making rescue slow going. Choppers were deployed to assist the ground crews. Efforts were impaired by the influx of media at the crash site.

Only a scant eleven passengers survived the initial accident. Five more died within the following week. The crash of American Air 1012 was described as one of the worst airline disasters in the history of aviation.

But in the initial moments immediately following the crash, only one question was present on the lips of friends, relatives and the country at large: who survived?

PART
II

March, 2002,

five months earlier

I

THE ELEVATOR DOORS PINGED OPEN. Dr. Gordon Brooks emerged onto the second-floor surgical wing of Mercy Hospital. He moved with quick steps down the hall, his leather shoes whispering softly on the institutional carpet. He passed a half-dozen operating suites. Yet it never occurred to him to wonder about any of the various surgical procedures taking place within.

The doctor was consumed with thoughts of the operation he would soon perform. In his mind's eye, he saw only the grayish yellow tumor deeply embedded in the patient's brain. He envisioned the gelatinous growth with its many tendrils reaching out to invade new, unexplored regions of the defenseless gray matter. The young woman's vision and equilibrium was already severely impaired. She would be dead in the very near future unless he could remove every last trace of the insidious tumor.

Gordon gripped the handle of his leather briefcase tighter. He pictured the surgery. He saw the exact point of entry through the skull, the circuitous approach taken to reach the tumor, then the delicate piece by piece cutting away of the mass.

He heard the whir of the drill. He smelled the smoke plume rising from the cauterizer. He saw the blood leaking onto the exposed brain. His concentration was absolute. So much so that he failed to notice the two women who called a greeting to him as he strode past the nurse's station.

Gordon headed directly to the doctor's locker room. Inside, he undressed, exchanging the well-tailored dove gray suit, matching shirt and burgundy tie for the comfortable, if somewhat shabby, warm-ups he always wore beneath the traditional green scrubs during surgery.

He sat down on a wooden bench and slipped his feet one-by-one into battered running shoes and tied the laces. A worried frown continued to dent his forehead. Only when he executed the final tug on the hastily fashioned bow, did he notice the death-grip he had on the laces.

He chuckled at himself. Contemplation of surgery always caused one emotion to rise to the surface and consume him completely. It was pure hate. He detested that tumor. It was the enemy that must be annihilated. He hated the growth for trying to first devastate, and then steal a human life.

He bent down and tossed one tasseled loafer then the other into the locker. The doctor stood and crossed the small room to a row of sinks.

Gordon inspected his face in the mirror. His red-rimmed eyes and gray skin clearly told the story of the previous night. Another fight with Alyssa. Although he easily recalled each individual aspect of the evening before --the cocktail party, the drive home, the argument, the yelling, the rage--try as he might, he simply couldn't remember what the actual problem had been.

He shrugged. Undoubtedly, it had just been more of the same. Something he had done, or didn't do. Something Alyssa wanted, or didn't want. Something he should have bought her. Who knew? Who even cared anymore?

Gordon shook his head to extinguish the vision of his wife's enraged countenance. He squared his sagging shoulders and flipped on the faucet. The slap of frigid water splashed on his face helped bring him back to the present.

Outside at the nurse's station, Rita Jenkins turned to Angela Harrison. Her friend sat tucked behind the desk on the opposite side of the counter. Rita scrutinized the woman as her eyes remained nailed to the locker room door. Angela's entire face was suffused with undisguised adoration and naked longing.

Rita was taken aback. She clucked her tongue. "You wear your heart on your sleeve."

Angela popped up in the seat, her hand fluttered to her mouth. "What did you say?"

"I said your feelings for Gordon Brooks are written all over your face."

"They are?"

"You bet. It would be impossible to miss. I had no idea you still had it so bad for him. Why didn't you tell me?"

The floor nurse smiled wistfully. "Guess I was just too embarrassed. After all, it's been so long, more than three years. I really should have been over him by now."

"Unfortunately, hearts don't punch a time clock, do they?"

Angela slowly shook her head back and forth. In a hushed voice, she replied, "No."

"I know you were hoping things would work out with the two of you."

"Yeah, I really was. But I guess he wanted something else."

The scrub nurse gave a derisive snort. "And look what he ended up with--that gold-digging bitch."

"That's what I've always hated about this situation," Angela confided. "If he had married a wonderful woman, someone who truly loved and cared about him, I would have understood it. But...her? She just wanted the money and prestige that goes with being married to such a prominent surgeon."

"I know," Rita agreed.

"It was so obvious to everyone, except of course, Gordon," Angela continued. "He was utterly blind-sided by her youth and beauty. I've got to give her that—she is one breath-taking female; vacuous as an empty room, but definitely something to look at. She played him like the proverbial fiddle and got what she wanted."

Rita gave a sharp bark of laughter. "You got that right. And every time I see him, he just looks more and more miserable."

"I know what you mean," Angela said. "He's about one of the nicest men you'd ever hope to meet."

At the sound of approaching footsteps, Rita said in a voice now tinged with sarcasm, "And speaking of nice guys, look at what the cat just dragged in."

Angela observed Dr. Richard Hapsburg striding toward them. She adopted the same sour expression as her friend.

"Hey girls, how's every little thing?" He sidled up next to Rita and gave her a pat. Even through a pair of old jeans and a set of scrubs, the nurse could feel the outline of his hand on her bottom.

Angela snatched a patient chart from the counter. She flipped it open and began reviewing its contents, hoping to avoid additional interaction. "Just fine, thanks."

Rita remained silent and edged farther down the counter.

Impervious to the negativity directed his way, Hapsburg asked, "So Cookie, am I going to get lucky today? Do I get to have you this afternoon?"

The nurse's jaw tightened. "The name's Rita. I am not your Cookie. If you are asking if I am going to scrub with you this afternoon, then the answer is yes."

"Good, good, good." He rubbed his palms together. The doctor leered as if she were standing before him in a skimpy bikini instead of a baggy green uniform. "Well then I'll catch you inside. Save your very best for me, doll." He threw her a wink, turned and strutted off down the hall.

Rita dusted the back of her scrubs with an open palm as if the simple motion alone might obliterate the memory of his groping hand. "That sack of shit."

Angela whispered, "Good grief. How does his wife stand it?"

"To heck with his wife. How do we stand it?"

Gordon was drying his face with a towel when the door swung open and Richard Hapsburg swept in with his usual flourish. The anesthesiologist went to his locker and began the same ritual Gordon had just completed. Dammit. Why hadn't he checked the schedule to see who would be working alongside him in the OR today? Gordon and Richard had disliked each other on sight; the enmity had only increased over the years.

From his vantage point in front of the gunmetal gray locker, Richard also regarded the other man and said, "You look like crap today."

Gordon wanted to lash out with an angry retort; he loathed this man. But they had to exist side-by-side for the next several hours. Keeping that in mind, he attempted a congenial smile. "Yeah, tough night."

Richard, with meticulous care, straightened a trouser leg on a padded coat hanger and placed it in his locker. He swaggered over to the sinks and propped one hip against the counter. "Feel as bad as you look?"

Gordon gave a half laugh. "Probably worse, if that is even possible."

Richard folded both arms across his broad chest and puffed up like a blow fish. "Yeah, my eyes have looked that red before."

The neurosurgeon studied his bloodshot eyes positioned behind the thick lenses of his glasses. "They do look pretty bad."

Richard elevated one bushy eyebrow in question. "Boozing?"

Gordon considered his words before replying. A propensity for gossip was known to be another one of Richard's fine qualities. "Some," Gordon hedged. "The night began with a cocktail party, then wine with dinner. You know how that goes."

A grunt of acknowledgement issued from between the anesthesiologist's lips. As Gordon finished up at the sink, Richard stared at him as if re-evaluating the other man.

The two doctors returned to their respective lockers. Richard squatted on the floor and rummaged around in the bottom of his locker. He found what he was searching for, then stood and held something out to the other doctor. Reflexively, Gordon took the item.

Richard suggested in a jovial voice, "Here, try this, a little hair of the dog as it were. Works for me every time."

Gordon stared at the flask, as horrified as if he held a live scorpion in his hand. Shock was the first emotion to register on his face. This was followed quickly by rage. "Alcohol? Are you out of your mind? You would actually drink before surgery?" He shoved the flask back into the other man's hands.

Richard, his face now a study in astonished bewilderment, backed away as if expecting a blow. "Well, I just thought ..."

Gordon flung his now-empty hand in the direction of the OR. "That young woman waiting in there is fighting for her life. She could die on the table under the best of circumstances. To even suggest that I would consider surgery while under the influence of anything is not only obscene, it is criminal."

Gordon advanced toward the anesthesiologist. He jabbed a rigid index finger mere inches from Richard's nose. His words exploded from his mouth in a tempest of fury. "I'll tell you what, you bastard. If I ever have reason to think you've been drinking before an operation of mine, by God, I will have you arrested on the spot. I'll report you to the AMA. I will personally see to it your license is pulled. You will never practice medicine again. Not anywhere, not anytime. Do you understand me, you worthless excuse for a human being?"

Richard nodded his compliance, still unable to speak. By now, his back was literally pressed up against the wall.

"Tell me that you fully understand what I just said to you. Tell me right now."

Richard found his voice. "Yes, I get it."

"Good," Gordon concluded decisively. He whirled around, slammed his locker door shut and stormed out of the room.

Richard dropped his still-startled gaze to the bottle he held in his hand. As the seconds ticked by, the stupefaction he initially felt metamorphosed into an almost palpable sense of indignant anger. "That sanctimonious prick. He can't talk to me like that. Just who does he think he is?" he muttered to himself as he returned to his locker, stowed the flask and kicked the door shut. His fists clenched and unclenched at his sides. He gazed at Gordon's locker and spoke to it as if it were the doctor himself. "I have had it with you, always thinking you are better than me. I'll get you someday, you condescending son-of-a-bitch. I'll make you pay. You will regret speaking to me like that for the rest of your life."

II

"AND TEN IS TWENTY." Doug Sanders enumerated with great care, dropping the money into the liver-spotted palm. "Now you make sure to come back and see us soon."

The elderly woman pocketed the money and reached for the small book of postage stamps lying on the counter. "You know I won't use anything on my letters but these precious cat stamps, since this looks just like my baby." She shuffled toward the door of the Coronado post office, then paused, hand on the knob. "The next time I'm here, you remind me to tell you more about my Bootsy."

Doug nodded at the eccentric old woman, one of their regulars. "You bet I will."

Vic, Doug's colleague, wandered in from the back room as the front door slid shut. "Let me guess. Bootsy? I swear, if I have to listen to one more adorable cat story, I am going to hang myself."

Doug ran his fingers through his hair and across his moustache. "Oh, it's not so bad. I kind of like working the front counter again when someone calls in sick. Gets me out of my office."

"Really, feel free to take over, anytime." Vic swung around and headed toward the break room. "Going to grab some coffee, want some?"

Doug flicked a glance at the wall clock. "No, thanks. I think I'll cut out a couple minutes early and go meet Alex at school."

Vic wandered back and leaned against the counter, coffee forgotten. "Sure, but before you go, will you please just tell me one thing? When are you going to finally ask Miss Too-Beautiful-for-Words out?"

"Vic, give it a rest."

"No. Just do it, for God's sake. All of us are getting tired of waiting. We're thinking about starting an office pool like we did last summer when Jan was way overdue with her first kid."

Doug punched his friend on the upper arm. "You guys need more work to do."

"The heck we do. Come on, make a move; ask her out on a real date. You two have been mooning around each other long enough. It's time for action."

Doug frowned, then acknowledged, "I really want to. I mean, I've been thinking about it for months. But ... it's complicated."

"Is it really that complicated?" Vic asked his boss. "You know that if you avoid it long enough, she'll end up with someone else. Women like Mandy don't stay on the open market for long. Is that what you want?"

Doug shook his head. "It's just that there hasn't been anyone in my life since Pam. Guess I'm just gun-shy."

"And I get that. But isn't she worth taking a chance on? It might work, or it might not. That's the risk we all take in life."

"You're right. I'll work on it. You'll be the first to know."

Vic smirked. "Just give me enough advance warning so I can win the pool, okay?"

"Gonna give me a cut?"

"You already know the answer to that," Vic rejoined. "Now get out of here."

Doug strolled along Orange Avenue, passed the Hotel Del Coronado. He looked in store windows, exchanged greetings with several people as he headed to the elementary school.

He thought about the conversation with Vic. He really did want to go out with Mandy. She was attractive and wonderful, funny and smart. He just had to get over this mental block. Marriages broke up all the time; he needed to move on.

At Village school, he spotted his son sitting on a stone bench with another boy. Both were hunched over, locked in rapt conversation. They peered with great interest at something held between them.

He closed in on the twosome. "Hey guys."

"Daddy." Alex jumped up and grasped Doug's forearm, his little face animated. "I'm so happy you're here. Guess what?"

Doug never gave the question a moment's thought. "What?"

"Dad, you've got to guess."

"But you know I'm no good at this game."

"Come on, just try."

"Okay, just this once." Doug feigned deep thought. "I know, you ate lizards for lunch."

Alex wrinkled his nose in consternation.

"No? That's not it? Well then, I've got it now: space aliens landed in the playground and kidnapped all the teachers. School is canceled indefinitely"

"Daddy," Alex said in that sing-song way that only small children can manufacture.

"Wrong again?" Doug squatted in front of his son. "I give up. What is it?"

"Sean traded me two X-Men cards for three Bulls," Alex told him, bouncing on the balls of his feet.

Standing alongside him, Sean's face broke into a gap-toothed grin as Alex elaborated, "The X-men are holograms. Look Dad, they're my favorites, Silver Surfer and Wolverine."

Doug took the cards and swiveled each one this way and that to appreciate the hologram's full range. "Pretty cool."

Doug returned the cards to his son then stood and straightened his pant legs. Sean dashed off toward the bike rack as Doug and Alex left the schoolyard.

"So what would you like to do for the rest of the afternoon, Bud? We could get your roller blades and go to the park, or grab your bat and hit some balls together."

Alex's face grew serious as he contemplated the various options. Doug couldn't resist reaching over and running a hand over Alex's new buzz haircut.

"I got it," Alex finally determined, swatting Doug's hand away. "Let's go play at the dunes."

"Great idea. We haven't been there in forever."

"Can we feed the birds?"

"You bet," Doug confirmed. "We'll stop by the store on the way and buy some day-old bread. The seagulls would definitely be bent out of shape if we didn't bring something for them."

Alex giggled. "Would they poop on our heads?"

Doug chuckled. "That's a definite possibility. Of course, they might anyway." He leaned over and kissed his son on the top of his head before Alex could swat him away, again.

Alex, positioned at the top of the sand dune, counted off the passing seconds. "Four Mississippi, five Mississippi, six Mississippi," he shouted, his hands cupped around his mouth like a megaphone.

Doug leaped forward as if hound dogs from hell were nipping at his heels. He landed sideways in the loose sand, momentarily lost balance, regained equilibrium, then bounded ahead. He sprinted the remaining four feet to the top of the dune. At the crest, he slapped his son's open palm, then collapsed on the sand, crumpling in a heap.

"Eight seconds," Alex declared with great enthusiasm. "Awesome Dad, it's a record, your best time yet."

Exhausted, Doug lay on his back, lungs heaving like fireplace bellows. "Get me a respirator, call 911. Do something quick, I'm dying."

His son flopped down beside him and peered into his face. "But you can't die now; it was a personal best, still two seconds behind me, but still a record. Just think, if we come back every week, by the end of the summer --""

"End of the summer nothing," Doug broke in still panting. He lifted himself onto his elbows. "No more dune running for this guy. I'm getting too old."

The boy snickered and sat back on his ankles. "Come on, Dad, you're doing great for fifty-two."

"What?" Doug gasped at the exaggerated age. "I'll give you fifty-two, young man."

He sprang like a jack-in-the-box at his son. Alex sped away on all-fours, racing to evade capture. Doug lunged forward and grabbed an ankle, tickling the bottom of one fleeing foot.

"Okay, okay, sixty-two," the boy amended, his words barely audible through the laughter, which bounced from dune to dune.

Doug released the foot, launching his son on a roll down the side of the sandy mound. At the bottom, Alex curled into a fetal position, wrapped his arms around his knees and laughed.

"Had enough?" Doug strained to be heard over the roar of the wind and the waves.

"Uh-huh."

"So we agree that not only am I the best dad in the world, but I am certainly the most youthful and physically fit?"

Alex grinned. His eyes darted around, weighing his options. "Um, um..."

From high atop the dune, Doug lifted his hands and positioned them like cat claws in the air. He wiggled his fingers, simulating tickling.

"Okay, you're the best."

"And the most fit?"

The boy nodded. Sand sprinkled down from his sun-bleached hair. "Absolutely."

Standing, Doug brushed the sand from his shorts and legs. "Well, now that we see eye-to-eye on that issue, I think I'll have to relax for a moment in the sun and think some lofty thoughts. Why don't you run around some more before we feed the birds."

Alex, by way of reply, rose and dashed off to scale yet another dune.

Doug slowly descended the sandy hill and wandered toward the water's edge. He lowered himself to the ground and folded his arms across his knees. His toes plowed deep trenches in the hard-packed sand.

The day was clear. Doug could even see the Coronado islands in the distance, something not easily done on overcast days. He raised a hand like a visor to shield his eyes from the glare of the setting sun and surveyed the sky. It was dotted here and there with cotton ball clouds.

He then studied the blue-green ocean and the myriad boats crisscrossing the horizon. There was everything from commercial fishing trawlers to massive Navy carriers. Best of all were the flamboyant sailboats, with their masts erect, sails billowing, skating across the water's surface like brightly colored water bugs.

Doug closed his eyes and laid back, palms flat on the hot sand. He reveled in the salty smell of the ocean air, the hypnotic song of the waves and the feather-like caress of the cool breeze. The heat from the sun drenched every inch of his bare skin and permeated his entire body. He drifted along like an untethered boat for several minutes. Doug heard Alex approach. He rolled over on his stomach, just as his son bounded from a dune, executed a karate kick in the air and yelled "ooh-argg."

"Hey, what ever happened to Geronimo?" Doug called as Alex scampered toward him.

"Huh?"

"Geronimo. That's what we used to yell when I was a kid."

"You did? So, who was he, a ninja?"

"Oh Lord God, never mind." Doug shook his head. "Ninja, indeed. I guess it's time to feed the seagulls."

The boy plopped down next to his dad and retrieved the sack of bread from beneath a beach towel. Alex, eagerness etched into his face, surveyed the horizon as well as the deserted beach. "See any?"

"Is that one over there?" Doug motioned to a point just above a nearby dune.

Alex tracked the trajectory of the hand and nodded. "Yep, I think so."

"Why not toss that guy a piece or two; that should bring the rest."

Alex jumped to his feet, grabbed a slice of stale bread and wandered across the sand. He positioned himself beneath the lone bird that soared perhaps fifteen or twenty feet above the ground. He broke off a small piece and flung the bread high into the air. The ocean breeze whipped it around and around. The silver-white gull dove straight for the spinning morsel and snagged it deftly with its opened beak. As if praising its own skill, the bird cawed boisterously, then hovered above Alex, expectant.

Doug grabbed the rest of the loaf and went to join Alex. Standing side-by-side, the two scanned their surroundings once again.

"There's one." Alex pointed toward the water.

"And two more are coming from down there," Doug added, gesturing to a distant point along the beach.

Within seconds, the sky above father and son was alive with circling gulls, dense as snowflakes during a blizzard. They swooped and dipped, colliding into one-another as they vied for the food. On the sand, clustered around their feet, squatted a dozen additional birds, snapping up crumbs that rained down from above.

The beach, recently so peaceful, now echoed with the shrill, plaintive cries of the airborne birds coupled with the strident chattering of those relegated to the ground.

Doug tossed several tidbits into the air, and then retreated to stand outside the circle. He watched his son as he interacted with the seagulls. As always, Alex wasn't merely feeding them, he was somehow bonding with the feathered creatures. It was something the father never fully understood.

Alex spoke to them constantly as he distributed the bread, murmuring soft encouragements that Doug was unable to discern over the din. Alex would hold his hand aloft and a bird would dive down and pluck the treat from his fingers, never biting his outstretched hand. When the boy dropped to one knee, the flock gathered close, snatching bread straight from his open palm. Time and time again, Doug had tried these feeding techniques, only to have the gulls ignore him or bite him hard enough to draw blood.

"Sorry guys, that's it for today," Alex told the gulls as he threw the final crust. Still squawking and scolding, the birds on the ground fluttered their black and gray flecked wings and strutted about, eyeing each other with suspicion.

The airborne contingent continued to circle a few moments longer. Eventually, the birds dropped to the sand to search for remnants.

Doug angled over to his child. "How do you do that?"

"Do what?"

"How do you have such a rapport with the birds?"

"I don't know what that word means, Daddy."

"Sorry Bud. What I mean is how do you get along with them so well? If I tried to feed them the way you do, they would make mincemeat out of me."

"Maybe that's because you're big."

"No, I don't think so. Even when I get down on my knees, they won't come to me like they come to you. What have you got going on that I don't?"

Alex scrunched up his face and thought about it. "I don't know...I don't think I have anything special. We just seem to get along. I really like them, maybe they know that."

Uttering a few mournful cries, the gulls finally dispersed, winging away in all directions. Following their lead, father and son collected their belongings and soon headed for home.

III

"**MAY ALMIGHTY GOD BLESS YOU** in the name of the Father, the Son and the Holy Spirit." Father John Larken stood at the altar and pronounced the age-old words. He made the sign of the cross in the air and added, "Now, let us go forth in peace to love and serve the Lord. Thanks be to God."

His final words of blessing rang through the massive church and the choir embarked on the closing hymn. John sang the familiar words and contemplated the assembled group. His heart sagged in his chest as he recalled the early days when simply looking upon his parishioners would fill him with such unspeakable joy, such a deep sense of purpose and fulfillment.

Those days were gone. Now, he only felt oddly empty, bereft. He felt his heart was merely a vacuum waiting to be filled with... what? He had no idea; he only knew something was deeply and drastically missing.

John, striving to shake off this all-too-familiar depression, allowed his gaze to sweep over the crowd. After all, this was why he had become a priest—to care for God's children.

He settled on one of his personal favorites, Deanna Gardner, who stood in her usual place in the first pew. With her perpetually exhausted face lifted toward heaven, she fervently worshipped God. Her hands were clasped together mere inches from her huge stomach, which looked more as if it contained a giant beach ball than a tiny infant waiting to be born. Filled with compassion for this young woman, John made a mental note to see if the church could help her in any way prior to the baby's arrival.

A glint of gold caught his eye and his attention was drawn to Brenda Reese positioned behind Deanna. The contrast between the two women was as arresting and undeniable as any the priest had ever encountered. Brenda was as rich as Deanna was poor, beautiful as the other was homely. To say nothing of spirituality, for Brenda was as apathetic to God as Deanna was devoted to Him.

Why did Brenda attend church anyway? Although John had pondered this question repeatedly, forever hoping to arrive at a reason that would indicate she possessed even a trace of love for God or the church, the answer was unfortunately always the same. Brenda, with her designer wardrobe, glamorous jewelry and most avant-garde coiffure attended mass for only one reason: to see and be seen. Even now, the priest could witness her avidly evaluating the crowd, undoubtedly selecting exactly whom she would grace with her company once the service was finally over.

Although John extended love to all his parishioners, despite their individual idiosyncrasies, actually liking some of them was a whole different matter.

Eventually, the hymn came to a close. John strode down the aisle and positioned himself just beyond the open doors to greet and exchange pleasantries with his parishioners as they left the sanctuary.

Twenty minutes later, John watched as the final few church members hurried along the sidewalk toward their cars. He headed for his office, intent on completing a stack of paperwork.

Halfway down the carpeted hall, he heard the familiar voice of Father Pat Flynn hailing him. John turned back to the partially open office door and peeked in. "Did you call me?" he asked the older priest, who was sitting in his leather chair. The desk before him was strewn with the usual scraps of paper, pyramids of books, candy wrappers, and empty soda cans.

Pat gave him an engaging smile. "Yes. I wanted to tell you that you did an excellent job this morning."

"Thanks. I keep telling you, I learned from the best."

"Indeed you did, my boy. Do you have a minute to talk with me?"

The younger man nodded. "Sure do. Just let me take off my vestments"

A moment later, John was back in the office, now dressed in casual light-blue slacks and a matching golf shirt. "Please sit." Pat beckoned to an armchair with a hand holding an unlit pipe.

John complied. He gazed pointedly at the cluttered desk. "You know, if cleanliness is really next to Godliness, you're in deep trouble. If the bishop hears about this, you're out."

Pat winked. "I won't tell, if you won't." He then extracted a tobacco pouch from beneath a pile of hand-outs from the morning service.

John's old friend and mentor embarked on the routine pipe-lighting ritual. He wondered how many times he had witnessed this procedure during recent years. Dozens? Hundreds? Each step was as familiar to John as the days of the week. He knew the precise quantity of aromatic tobacco necessary to fill the bowl and the exact amount of time it took to adequately tamp it down before lighting.

There was an orderliness to the act he found strangely comforting, not unlike the touch of his tattered terry cloth robe at the end of a long day.

John knew additional conversation would not ensue until the ritual was complete. He settled back and considered the large window behind Pat's desk. Although the morning had been awash in crisp sunlight, ominous gray clouds now loomed on the horizon. He suspected the siege, predicted by all local weather forecasters, would commence in fewer than ten minutes.

Pat ignited a silver lighter. John's attention was yanked back to his friend.

When had Pat's hair gone so gray? When John had first come to St. Tim's, Pat's abundant hair had been black. Now, though still thick, it was shot through with gray, showcasing much more salt than pepper. Even the small tufts of hair sprouting from his ears were as gray as the clouds threatening in the distant sky.

John had never given the priest's advancing age much thought. Now he grew acutely aware of the deep webbed lines framing Pat's eyes and limning his mouth. The old priest's skin was nearly translucent.

A flicker of concern flared in John's heart. He leaned forward, intending to ask if everything was all right. Pat puffed up a cloud of blue smoke and swung his head toward John. "You look as if you've seen a ghost hovering right above my very head."

John chuckled in relief. His old friend was fine. His imagination had just gotten the better of him. "No, no ghosts."

The priest sucked on his pipe, then waved it in the air. "Not even the Holy Ghost?" His deep black eyes twinkled with mirth. "Now that would be something, indeed."

"Too true. But the only thing showcased above you right now is a ton of dark clouds. They appear to be heading this way."

Pat flicked a glance over one shoulder. "And so they do." Parking the stem between his teeth, he drew on his pipe a few more times until satisfied. The following words, though slightly muffled, sounded infinitely more serious. ""I've been worried about you lately, son. I have a feeling that something is wrong. Actually, I was hoping you'd come and tell me what the problem was but..." his words trailed off, leaving the sentence unfinished.

"I would have talked to you about it except," John hesitated, at a loss for words. "I had no idea what to say. I don't really know what the problem is, myself. If I didn't know better, I would say I was suffering from some sort of mid-life crisis."

The older man tapped the pipe against his bottom teeth, then spoke around its stem. "If only it were that simple. Then I'd know all you needed was a snazzy red sports car or a shapely young blonde and you'd be all better just like that." Arcing one hand through the air, he snapped his fingers together to underscore his point.

The elder priest gestured toward a manila folder lying open on his desk. "I was reviewing your file earlier today. I hadn't had occasion to look at it since you first came to us several years ago."

He swung a foot onto his desktop. "You know John, you and I have spent an untold number of hours sitting just like this in my office talking. We've discussed everything from the Church's stance on birth control to whether we should have solid chocolate or malted-milk eggs at the Easter picnic. But it occurred to me, we've never really chatted about your life...I mean your early life, prior to joining the priesthood. And your file doesn't appear to offer much along those lines either. Not where you were brought up, your family, siblings, nothing."

John stiffened, his throat constricted. He could feel himself pulling back, closing in on himself like a home where shutters are being drawn closed against a pending storm. He had avoided discussing his past with everyone for years. Now, he knew with an unflagging certainty there was no escape. "No, guess we never have."

"For some reason, I can't imagine why," Pat commented, his own brand of wry sarcasm lurking within every word, "I get the most distinct impression you'd rather not discuss this."

John looked down and picked at a cuticle, visibly retreating. "No, I would really prefer not. In fact, I was hoping you and I could talk about Deanna Gardner for a minute. I think..."

Pat's left foot slammed to the floor. He sat forward and impaled John with a look. "Son, remember me? I'm your friend, I care about you. Frankly, if just mentioning your past can trigger this type of reaction, then this is something we need to talk about this very minute."

His voice was implacable. "Honestly John, right now you look like a totally different person --'""

"That's because I was a totally different person back then," John cut in sharply. Then reconsidering the statement, he amended, "Or maybe I was actually the same person, but my life was just so terribly different."

"I suspect your second analysis is probably a little closer to the truth." Pat's pipe went out. He retrieved the lighter from his desk, flicked it open and spun the wheel. He drew in air, seducing the flame toward the bowl. Through a billow of smoke he said, "Why don't you tell me about it."

Silence settled over the room. John sat still, knocking the knuckles of both hands together. He focused on the blank wall next to him as if it might miraculously offer up a new script from which to read. Yet, no new scenario was forthcoming. Instead, the shifting patterns of sunlight outside the window caused the textured surface of the white wall to come seemingly alive.

Vague images of various people from John's past were offered up. John discerned his father. There was the familiar widow's peak, the puffy dark pouches beneath both eyes, the slack skin around the jaw line.

The filtered light shifted. He imagined he saw Bridget--the impish grin, the cavalcade of freckles marching across her upturned nose. Abruptly, the dark bloated clouds outside the window coagulated. The sun disappeared. Bridget's vague visage vanished.

In the subsequent gloom Greg's face emerged ever so faintly on the wall. John strained to make it out. He thought he caught a glimpse of the curly mop of black hair and the equally dark Irish eyes. Then the impression was gone.

Pat gave a short cough. Determination was clearly etched in the older priest's face.

John resigned himself to the task of unearthing the past. He took in a deep breath, then exhaled audibly in the silent room. "There is nothing good about this story."

Pat offered a crisp nod of affirmation.

"There were five of us in my family: my father, mother, a kid brother and sister." John spoke in a flat voice. "We lived in a lower-middle class suburb in South Boston. My parents worked on an assembly line in a local factory.

"From as far back as I can remember, my father drank. It wasn't so bad when I was very young; back then, we kids thought it was more funny than not. Dad would act silly and we would all laugh--it seemed relatively harmless. Yet, as we got older, he drank more and more and it wasn't funny any longer. Like so many, he was a mean drunk. We soon learned to avoid him when he had that 'look'. And on the nights he stayed out late, the three of us would actually hide under the bed, so he couldn't get to us when he finally made his way home."

John chuckled, a sad sound utterly void of humor. "It seems hard to imagine now but amazingly, it actually worked. He never did find us under that bed; it was as if he had literally forgotten we even existed at all. I can still remember how good it felt under there, dust bunnies and all, because we were safe. Bridget, Greg and me, our little bodies flattened on the floor, pressed up against one another like sardines in a can, our noses almost touching the sagging bedsprings.

"The only problem was, even though we couldn't see him, we could hear him clearly. For a long time, verbally abusing our mother seemed to satisfy him, but after a while, it evidently wasn't enough. The three of us would lie beneath that bed and listen as he would systematically beat the hell out of her.

"One time Greg, who was just a scrawny little runt of a kid, couldn't take it anymore. He scrambled out from under the bed and tried to defend her." John faltered in his narrative, remembering. With the words came the agonizing recollection: Greg's pinched little face, white as a stick of chalk, the trembling lower lip, the clenched fists poised scant inches from his narrow chest mimicking a boxer's stance. John dragged a hand down his face as if hoping to wipe away the painful memory, then summed up in a husky voice. "Greg didn't have a chance; my father broke his arm in two places and his face was nearly unrecognizable for weeks.

"When we grew older and couldn't squeeze under the bed anymore, we took to the streets, trying to stay out later than he did. Once he had passed out, we were safe, at least until the next time he went on a bender. Bridget, who was two years younger than me, did what any teenage girl would do placed in that circumstance--she found solace in boys, usually those much older than she was.

"Of course, she ended up pregnant. Somehow, Dad found out and beat her so badly that night, she had to be hospitalized. As a result she lost the baby. A week later, she ran away from home. I never saw her again." John's voice cracked and he barely managed to add, "My beautiful little sister. I loved her so much..."

Tears rolled down John's face. He was oblivious to the pungent pipe smoke wafting through the small office or the patter of raindrops striking the windowpane like a thousand miniature feet tap-dancing across the glass.

"When I was eighteen, the night before I was to graduate from high school, my father came home early, drunker and meaner than I had ever seen him before. I was at the kitchen table, Mom was pressing my white graduation gown. Greg was out.

"Dad immediately started in on Mom. Just yelling at first, but I knew it was going to get bad...real bad...real fast. When he finally went for her, I jumped on his back. He tossed me off. I was fairly strong for my age, yet he threw me like I was nothing more than a rag doll. I slammed into a wall, fell to the floor. I was dazed, nearly unconscious.

John stopped dead in his narrative. In the darkly shadowed room, both men sat still and silent as the furniture. One waited patiently, while the other searched for the courage to continue.

John slouched deeper in his seat. He gripped the chair arms, his knuckles as white as the office walls. He released a sigh of the most infinite agony. "I don't know why that particular night was different from all the rest. My mother had finally had enough. Something just snapped.

"While he still had his back to her, she yanked the cord from the wall and hit him over the head with that steam iron. He went down immediately, collapsed to the floor in a heap. His hair sizzled; his scalp burned. She kept pounding him again and again, grunting with every strike.

"It was a visceral, animal sound; I had never heard anything like that before. I finally crawled over and pulled that gory thing from her hand. By then, his head was completely pulverized. He was dead. Blood was everywhere. It pooled on the floor. It dripped from Mom's hair. It had splattered all over my graduation gown. I remember both of us just stared for the longest time at that gown draped over the ironing board. The fabric was so white and the blood was so red. Oh God Pat, the blood was so red..."

John's words faded away. His eyes glazed. He pictured the horrific scene, as perfectly preserved as if stored under a glass dome all these years. He groaned, his voice now as distant as his gaze. "I had never seen so much blood in my life. I can still vividly recall the metallic smell of it mixed with seared flesh."

"And then," Pat prompted.

John jerked back to the present. He composed himself and went on. "A few weeks later, I had to testify about what happened that night. They ultimately released my mother, but she was never really the same again.

"The following day I left Boston. The truth was I just couldn't handle much of anything anymore. I was done. I had to get away. I ended up in New York. My uncle and aunt took me in and I lived there while I went to college."

Pat's face mirrored the misery reflected in the other man's eyes. He lit his pipe once more and puffed. He flapped a hand to wave away the smoke. "And your brother Greg?"

John continued to stare at the wall. A slight shudder, as quick as a lightening flash, passed through him. "Dead, killed in a car crash about a year after my dad."

Pat winced at the unexpected answer. Could this story get any worse? Reluctantly, he posed the final question, "Your mother?"

John shrugged, a gesture indicating utter defeat. "Oh I guess she's probably still in Boston. Like I said, never really the same after my father's death. But even more than that, she never got over me going to seminary. Only thing she hates more than God is the church. My father was the one who was brought up Catholic.

"When I moved out West, I sent her my phone number and address, just in case. I think as far as she is concerned all of her children are dead." With that, John's eyelids slid shut. Spent, he dropped his head against the back of the chair.

Pat placed the pipe in a clay ashtray, then entwined his fingers together on his lap. He reflected on all he had just heard. Intuitively, he had known John was carrying around a burden, even suspected it was linked to his family. However, he would never have guessed how truly heavy the weight had been. Now he knew, and there was a part of his heart, albeit a small part, that fervently wished he'd never asked.

He glanced out the window, now blurred by trickling rainwater. The cloudburst would soon subside, leaving everything fresh and clean in its wake. Maybe this time spent with John would pass similarly. Perhaps his soul would be purified through the telling of the terrible and long-suppressed story.

Pat licked his lips and asked in a hushed voice, "Why did you decide on the priesthood, son?"

John ran his hand distractedly through his brown hair. "At the time, I thought I was doing it for all the right reasons: a love for God, a desire to do his work on earth, a dedication to the church. But I've been thinking about it lately. I don't know if my motivations were ever that pure. Sometimes I wonder if I wasn't trying to create a new type of extended family."

"Wouldn't be the first time. The only problem is," the elder priest proffered in a slightly stronger tone, "It never works. The church can't fix a defective family any more than it can heal hurts from the past. It can only be what it is--the church--nothing more. If you ask more of it, you are setting yourself up for a fall--you will always come up empty."

John rocked forward, interest quickened. "Yes, that's exactly how I've been feeling lately--empty."

"I'm not surprised. Frankly, I'm only surprised it's taken this long. When a person has unrealistic expectations of anyone or anything--a wife from a husband, a child from a parent, a priest from the church--it usually falls apart pretty fast."

John steepled his fingers in front of his lips. "It's probably been degenerating for a while. I just refused to see it."

"Could be. Thought about leaving, perhaps doing something else with your life?"

"Yes. I wonder if I belong elsewhere. It's just that I've been feeling so, so..."

"Empty."

John nodded. "Right."

"You know I'd hate to lose you, son, that goes without saying. But if you decide to leave, I want it to be for the right reason. As long as your motivation for anything is based in the past, you've lost the race before you're even out of the blocks. Trust me, you could look any number of places for a cause to champion or even a person or persons to love and if your heart is in the wrong place, you will absolutely always remain--"

"Empty?" John completed. A slight smile had finally broken through the mask of anguish.

Relieved to feel the tension ebbing from the room, Pat emitted a short chuckle. "That's right, my lad, and I'm glad to see you're listening to all of this sage advice."

"Oh believe me, I am hanging on every single utterance." The younger priest referenced the desk with the wave of a hand. "I would have taken word-for-word notes, but knew I'd never find a pen in that mess."

The two laughed way out of proportion to what the joke actually merited. The humor was such a welcome relief.

"What I'd like to do," Pat finally suggested, "Is to get together on a regular basis. We need to talk this thing out and get to the bottom of all your thoughts and feelings once and for all. "

John's expression, strictly by force of habit, instantly altered. His face took on a guarded, wary look. Invisible armor was settling back into place. The transformation was not lost on Pat. The old priest rushed to reassure his young friend. "John, it will be all right. You've already told me the story. There's nothing to hide anymore."

John relaxed. The apprehension vanished as quickly as it had appeared. "I'm sorry, Pat, I guess that's just a knee-jerk reaction."

"I understand. Now why don't you go get your calendar and we'll schedule a time to meet."

As John walked out, the elder priest leaned back, feeling distraught. He knew he was advocating the right course of action and truly hoped he could help his friend. Yet, Pat remained plagued by the knowledge that after all was said and done, he might just lose him. Quite possibly, Pat could successfully counsel one of the finest men he'd ever known right out of the priesthood.

IV

THE PEARL-GRAY LIMOUSINE PULLED up to the curb and rolled to a stop. The uniformed chauffeur hopped from the driver's seat and opened the rear door, swinging it wide.

Shea Lansing emerged into the dark night and thanked the driver. At the front door of the white-stucco house, she fumbled with keys, then rushed inside. In quick succession, she punched in the four-digit security code on the wall keypad and simultaneously flipped on three light switches with an upward sweep of one hand.

She stood in the foyer and called, "Clyde, Clyde, sweetheart, where are you?" She heard a familiar thump from the bedroom and took several steps forward. She spotted him charging through the doorway. He raced toward her, green eyes still slit narrowly from sleep, yet with his long black tail held high in its usual question-mark position.

Shea bent down to scoop the little black cat up in her arms. "Oh baby, I missed you, I missed you so much," she told the cat. She hugged him tight and buried her face in his dense, velvet-soft fur, nuzzling his neck. She stroked him with one hand as he kneaded her shoulder with his puffy black paws. He purred loud as a locomotive. Eventually, he clambered to get down. Shea placed him on the gleaming tile floor. In a flash he was gone, just a blur of black fur scampering off in the direction of the kitchen.

Shea laughed at the cat's predictable antics. She knew exactly where he was headed. Delighted to participate in the game, she walked down the short connecting hall. Clyde was waiting for her on the kitchen counter poised mere inches from his food dish. He spied her approach and hunkered down. The cat began ravenously devouring his dry cat chow.

"I know, I know, you poor thing, you're starving to death. You haven't eaten in days," she commiserated in an appropriately empathetic voice. She patted his back and he crunched, still purring.

For several minutes, Shea stood there stroking the cat in contentment. She had missed Clyde more than she would ever have thought possible. "You know, you are just a cat. Seriously, not all that special," Shea told him. She ran a hand lightly along his arched back and down the length of his tail, which coiled on the counter behind him.

At her words, Clyde paused mid-munch, cocked his head in her direction, blinked, then returned to his food. She folded her arms on the counter as her mind drifted to the first time she'd seen Clyde.

Shea had been on her way to a photo session. Traffic had made her late. The last thing she needed was to pull over where a gang of neighborhood kids squatted alongside a sign. It read "Kats for Sale." There were five kids and four kittens. Clyde was the smallest and by far, the most energetic of the felines. He pounced on the other kittens, leaped over the edge of the brown cardboard box, and attacked the frayed laces of one boy's tennis shoe. His jet black fur reminded her of Bonnie, the next-door neighbor's cat when she was growing up.

Shea mentally marshaled all the standard arguments. She told herself that pets were a nuisance, her lifestyle wasn't conducive to animals and she had enough responsibility already. Nothing worked.

Even her best argument of all--the fact that she didn't even particularly like cats—tanked. The moment she pressed the tiny black bundle to her cheek, it was over. Shea couldn't get the five dollars out of her wallet fast enough. The kitten was immediately dubbed Clyde, in memory of Bonnie.

Of course, she was more than marginally late for the photo shoot. That client never did hire her again. Tough. Clyde had been worth every penny of lost revenue, and then some.

Now, she leaned on the kitchen counter and watched as the eating ritual came to a close. This cat meant everything to her. Perhaps someday she'd value another person the way she did Clyde. That may, or may not be, in the cards. It sure hadn't been up to this point. Clyde still remained the only living creature Shea had ever really loved.

"Done?" she asked the cat as he took a final bite. Clyde stood straight and swung his tail skyward. He sauntered over to her, touched noses, then leaped to the floor and headed for the hall. A creature of habit, she knew he was off to her bedroom to groom himself on top of her bed.

Shea paused in the doorway to yawn and stretch expansively. Only now did she fully appreciate how bone-tired she was. It had been a long and grueling two days.

She returned to the front door to retrieve her bag and reengage the security system. The message machine light flashed on her desk.

Damn that thing, she thought, the happy expression of moments earlier rapidly drained from her face. She peered closer. Twelve messages in only two days.

Sighing in fatigue and exasperation, Shea picked up a notepad and flopped down in a nearby chair. She punched the play button. Minutes later, her message list was complete. Yawning again, she headed for her bedroom.

Shea thought about the phone messages as she prepared for bed. Most concerned pending jobs or personal appearances; others dealt with the latest negotiations regarding the new sportswear line that would carry her name. Two messages were from Connor Spate. He wanted to see her.

Seriously, how many times had she already turned him down when he asked her out? Her policy was fairly clear: Shea never dated anyone she worked with.

She bent over the marble sink and splashed water on her face. Uncharacteristically, she giggled, remembering Connor's humorous messages. He was awfully cute. But she reminded herself that rules were rules. And despite the popular notion, they really were not meant to be broken.

Models should never date photographers. That was that. Of course, the fact that Shea never dated anyone was not something she was willing to think about. The next time he called she would just have to explain her policy one more time and hope it finally sunk in.

Shea dismissed all further thought of Connor Spate, meandered over to her bed, pulled down the coverlet and climbed in between the crisp sheets. Immediately, four tiny feet paced up the length of the mattress toward the headboard. Shea smiled in the darkness. Clyde perched alongside her on the pillow and peered down into her face. She lifted the sheet, then extended a hand to stroke the compact bundle of fur next to her. The silent room was filled with his loud purr.

Clyde took a single step forward, circled once, then flopped down. His back snuggled against her chest and his head rested alongside hers on the lace-trimmed pillowcase. She tucked a hand beneath his plump belly and rested her cheek against his vibrating neck. She had missed the comfort of this warm little body during the past two nights.

Suddenly a thought struck her from out of the blue and she chuckled into Clyde's fuzzy pointed ear. It twitched crazily. *What fun people would have if they knew the only male Shea Lansing had ever shared a bed with was an eight-pound black cat.*

The day dawned bright and sparkling over the Pacific Ocean. By eight o'clock, the mercury had pushed into the high seventies; the dusting of dew on bushes and grass had long since dried. A balmy breeze fluttered through the open office window, carrying with it the noisy chatter of birds gossiping in distant trees.

Coffee mug in hand, Shea sat at her desk. It was piled high with textbooks and old newspapers. She enumerated the various tasks she must complete that day. With one final notation, she perused the list in its entirety. She grimaced. Where was she going to find the time to do all this? The term paper for her microeconomics class alone would eat up the entire afternoon.

The fingertips of her left hand drummed nervously on the desktop while she tried to work out a strategy. Thank God she'd given up smoking, or she'd be reaching for a pack and lighting up this very moment.

Like so many models, Shea had picked up the habit a couple of years ago in an effort to stay thin. After a few months, she'd given it up. If she had to risk her health to keep a career, Shea was in the wrong business. The decision was one she never regretted. Yet, when stress was particularly high, she found herself thinking about smoking a whole lot more than normal.

Shea pushed her chair back from the desk and tossed the list back onto its smooth wood surface. First things first.

In the bathroom, she clipped her hair into a ponytail and rubbed sunscreen into her skin. She caught a glimpse of herself in the full-length mirror on the bathroom wall. A hoot of laughter cut into the silence. She had on grungy running shoes, a pair of faded yellow gym shorts and a washed-out T-shirt that had definitely seen better days. With her hair pulled back, no makeup and sunscreen still drying on her cheeks, she looked like the "before" picture in an ad for self-improvement. It only got better when she jammed a navy blue Angels baseball cap on the top of her head and yanked down the red bill.

"Oh sure…, a face that could inspire poets," she quoted aloud. Just last week, a writer for the LA Times had used that expression to describe her. Of course, the statement was silly; but now, it was down-right preposterous.

If he could only see me now, Shea thought as she walked toward the foyer. He would realize that in this particular case, poets could only be inspired by buckets of makeup, great lighting and at least a half-dozen filters on the camera lens.

"Hold down the fort Clyde, I'll be back soon," she called out to her cat for no apparent reason. She switched on the security system, then hurried to the front door.

Shea stepped outside and slammed straight into Connor Spate's chest. He was standing right there on her front stoop. One hand was held in the air, obviously preparing to knock.

Astonished even more by his presence than the unexpected collision, Shea leaped back. "What are you doing here?"

He appeared equally surprised. "Well, I just came to see if we could perhaps spend the morning together."

Incredulity rapidly replaced shock. "Are you kidding? What were you thinking? Why didn't you call?"

He grinned boyishly. His closely cropped beard bunched up on either side of his mouth. There was a hint of a dimple. "I called a couple of times. Didn't you get my messages?"

"Yeah, I did but, but --"" Shea cut off her own words mid-sentence. She darted a frantic glance at the green light blinking on the foyer wall. *Dearest God, in seconds, it would flash to red and those darn alarms would go off. The police would be summoned. It would be a nightmare.* "Look, I don't have time for this. I must go running right now. Want to come?"

"Well," he pondered the question. Connor glanced down at his shorts and shirt as if he had all the time in the world to contemplate this conundrum.

Shea flung her hands out in frustration. She conjured images of speeding police cars and wailing sirens. "Come on, make up your mind. Yes or no," she demanded, her voice clearly reflecting her outrage.

"Yes."

"Good." This situation was anything but good. She yanked the door shut behind her.

Shea waited on the walkway as Connor shed his shoes and socks and left them on the stoop. Side by side, the two ambled across the sand to the water. They headed south, skirting the shoreline. Shea set the pace. She didn't know if he was a runner or not and frankly, didn't give a rat's ass. Just showing up at her home like that? How did he get her address? And how had he gotten through the guarded gate? She paid a lot of money to ensure her own safety. This was something she must look in to.

Connor remained silent as they ran. The crash of waves and the pounding of feet on hard-packed sand were the only sounds surrounding them. Shea had counted on her standard six-mile run. However, the increasingly labored quality of Connor's breathing caused her to cut it short.

"Are we finally stopping? Is this it? Are we done?" Connor panted, his voice coming in sharp, ragged gasps.

Shea slowed to a rapid walk. "Uh-huh." She pulled the baseball cap off her head, wiped her sweaty brow with a forearm and clamped the hat back on her head. She blew out a puff of air and cast a glance in his direction.

His admittedly handsome face was beet red and streaming with sweat. The front of his sky blue T-shirt was entirely soaked. He looked like a candidate for the emergency room. "I figure this is good enough for today."

"Bummer. I was hoping we'd go a couple more miles -- I was just hitting my stride." At her dubious look, his face reconfigured into the same grin he'd tried to win her over with earlier. But this time it worked. Her initial annoyance had dissipated.

The two walked and talked for a long time. He told her about the assignment he had flown in for; in turn, she described the job she had just completed. The conversation was relaxed and easy, since they knew most of the same players.

As they drew near her house, he asked, "Earlier, when we were outside your front door, you said you must go out running. What's that all about? Do you actually enjoy running or only do it because of work?"

Shea, who had been inspecting the path in front of her for unusual shells, considered the question. What a curious thing to ask. Most men wouldn't have given it a second thought, no less inquire about it. "Sure, I need to stay in shape, but I get that more from working out on weights at the gym three times a week and doing yoga. More than anything, I run because I need to be out here." She arced one hand out in a half circle to reference their surroundings. "See, I never lay in the sun and walking takes too long, so in order to spend the time I need to be alone in this environment, running is really the only option."

He looked around them. "I still don't get it."

Shea decreased her pace and contemplated her reply. So many thoughts, ideas and emotions constantly filled her mind. She never discussed them with anyone--not her few women friends, and certainly not men. She never allowed herself to get that close to any man. And Connor Spate of all people. Why would she make herself vulnerable to him? The answer was simple: she wouldn't.

With every intention of offering some watered-down response, Shea opened her mouth. To her considerable astonishment, she found herself speaking the truth. "Spending time here helps me keep everything in perspective. Just look at this," she instructed. Facing the ocean, she spread both arms out wide as if to encompass all that lay before her. "Look at how huge all of this is, how great and magnificent the world is. By comparison, we are nothing, really nothing at all.

"All of us are just these little insignificant creatures walking around on this earth. We want so much to believe we have great value, but we just don't." She allowed her arms to go limp and flop back to her sides like broken wings.

Connor came to a stop alongside her. Their shoulders nearly touched. "True, but why do you feel you need to remind yourself of it?"

Shea frowned and bit the edge of her lower lip, now even more befuddled. She groped for the right words. The idea had always been so clear in her mind, yet expressing it aloud was proving far more difficult than ever imagined. "Because of the way my life is..." Her voice trailed off, the frown intensified. Shea studied the water as if the words she searched for were lurking just beneath the next foam-capped wave.

Connor waited patiently. He liked the way their individual shadows puddled together at their feet.

She lifted a shoulder. "Because everyone is always going on and on about how gorgeous, how photogenic, how perfect I am. Blah, blah, blah. You know the drill. You've heard it enough. You've seen it happen. Sycophantic people who don't know me at all are constantly fawning over me because I'm so famous, supposedly SO beautiful."

"But Shea, you really are that beautiful." He put forth the thought simply as a statement of fact, without guile.

She shrugged. "So what? Who cares? Does that mean I'm a good person, does it mean I have a good heart? No. It doesn't mean jack. And what's more, did I do anything remarkable to earn it? The way I, or anyone else for that matter, looks is just the luck of the draw. It's DNA. My appearance doesn't have one damn thing to do with me personally. Not one thing at all."

She sighed. "It's just the way our world is. So often people bestow value and give credit where it just isn't due."

Still baffled by why she was even telling him these things, she turned to him for confirmation. "Can you understand what I'm trying to say? I mean, at all?"

His forehead wrinkled in concentration. "I've never given it much thought before, but I might see your point."

Shea lowered herself to the sand, drew her knees up to her chest and encircled both legs with her arms. "When I've been wrapped up in that synthetic world we both travel in too long, I need to come back here. I need to get grounded, anchored once more in what really matters. Connor, this is what's real. This is genuine beauty, beauty that lasts.

"God forbid, if I ever started taking the modeling or fashion world or even myself too seriously, everything I believe in, everything I am would just cease to exist. I'd be lost, probably forever."

He sank down beside her and unconsciously folded his body into the identical position. Connor tossed her a cocky look. "Then you'd start thinking you were the cat's ass like so many other models?"

Shea burst out laughing. "That's 'super' model to you, dude. And in no time at all, I'd feel compelled to start putting smart-ass photographers like you in your place."

"Oh, that's about all I need." He flicked sand at her. In retaliation, she scooped up a handful of damp sand and tossed it onto his bare feet.

She scooted a few yards away and flopped down on her stomach. He followed. Once again, he mirrored her posture. He laid flat on the sand, arms crossed over one another, with his chin resting on his forearms. "For what it's worth," he said, speaking in a low, serious voice. "I have been watching you, really watching you, for a long time, now. When I look at you, I think I honestly see you, the person inside. Kind of sounds like some cheap, pick-up line, doesn't it? Well, it's not, I mean it.

"Sure, when I study you through a lens, I see a breathtaking, incredibly photogenic, woman. If I told you anything different, I would be a liar. But when I am just talking to you, like when we were walking earlier and right now, I think I see you, the real you inside, beneath all that beauty. Know what I mean?"

Shea lifted her head and offered a slow nod of affirmation. "Maybe."

Connor sifted a handful of sand through his fingers. He plucked out a broken shell and examined the jagged edge with great interest. "Jesus Shea, with so many of the female models I work with, what you see is what you get. That's all there is. Sure, they have faces or bodies that could easily stop traffic, but that's it. There's absolutely nothing beneath the surface. There truly is no one home. And for some men that's enough.

"For years, it was enough for me. I'd parade all these gorgeous creatures around town, thinking I was such a stud. I was so impressed with myself. You know the standard macho bullshit. I was totally into it. And where did that get me? Nowhere, just a life full of nothing relationships. I'm done with that gig.

"I want more from a woman, more from a relationship. See, I think I might be able to find that with you. That's why I keep pursuing you, despite the fact that you've done everything in the book, short of spitting right in my face, to turn me down."

"That was next on my list," she uttered straight-faced, her quiet voice as serious as her expression.

Connor slapped his forehead. "God help me, how much more can one man take?" He brushed a layer of fine sand off one arm. "Come on Shea, take a chance. I like you, it's really that simple. I think you might even like me just a little. Couldn't we just spend some time together, hang out, have some fun, get to know each other better? Is the fact that we might have to work together sometime really that big of a damn deal?"

She thought it over, trying to be realistic and fair, yet reluctant to abandon her original resolve.

As the moments passed, Connor continued to stare at her with those incredible blue eyes. Eventually, her resolve weakened, then fell apart all together. Finally she conceded, "No, I guess not."

He sprung up on his elbows. "Great. Then how about tonight? I have to work this afternoon as you know. I should be done by six. We could have dinner together. How about it?"

"Just one question, and I warn you in advance, your answer will literally make or break this whole thing."

"Okay, shoot."

Shea favored him with a long, speculative look. "How do you feel about cats?"

"That's easy--I'm crazy about them. Matter of fact, I have two of my own. A fat tiger named Kodak and a little tabby named Flash."

That did it. Shea smiled. "Perfect. You pick the restaurant; I'll be ready to go at seven."

PART III

May, 2002

I

DOUG SQUINTED IN THE DIM overhead light to verify the amount-due on the electric bill. He scribbled the figure on the check and signed his name. The monthly bill-paying process was finally complete.

He consulted the wall clock. "Alex," he called toward the staircase. It's eight-fifteen, better brush your teeth and get ready for bed."

"Okay, Daddy."

The man sighed, concerned anew by the flat, lack-luster sound of his son's voice. *What was wrong with him?*

He went into the kitchen and stood at the stainless steel sink and washed the dinner dishes. He considered a constellation of possibilities for the odd behavior. Alex wasn't sick, he seemed to be getting along well with his friends, and wasn't in any kind of trouble at home or school. Then what was it?

He rinsed the dishes in near scalding water. *Damn, he should have bought those yellow rubber gloves from the grocery store last week.* He propped the plates and glasses in the white plastic rack on the counter.

Samson meandered into the compact kitchen. The dog began licking the bottom of his empty food bowl with great enthusiasm. His silver chain collar clanked against its metal side.

Doug looked down at him. "Sorry chum, you know you've already been fed tonight." Sam gazed at Doug forlornly with dark, soulful eyes. The lab returned to the dish, now relentlessly nudging it around the floor with his nose.

Doug scooped up a handful of silverware from the bottom of the sink and dropped forks and spoons into their slot on the rack. "Never say die," he commented to the dog before he rescued the bowl. He placed it in the now-empty sink and ran water in it. Unrequited, Sam wandered away as Doug went to the base of the stairway calling, "You ready?"

"Yeah."

The floorboards beneath the threadbare carpet creaked like old bones with every step Doug took on the stairs. In Alex's room, he sat down on the edge of the bed beside his son. "Get all that homework done?"

The boy rolled over onto his stomach, scrunched under the covers and shoved his arms beneath the pillow. "Yep."

Doug switched off the bedside lamp; the room was immediately drenched in gray haze, now lit only minimally by the light burning in the family room below. The bedtime ritual went as usual. Doug rubbed his son's back for several minutes while they chatted about inconsequential things. After a while, he leaned over, kissed his son on the back of the head and left.

Downstairs, Doug noticed Alex's backpack sitting on the edge of the couch. He grabbed the bag and yanked the zipper open as he returned to the kitchen. He fished out the X-Men lunch box and Alex's corrected homework mingled together with a handful of parent notices. The last sheet was a monthly calendar of classroom events. And there it was—the reason for Alex's strange behavior.

The second-grade class was planning a gala Mother's Day event. The only problem was, Alex didn't have a mother.

"Shit, why didn't you remember?" the man castigated himself aloud in the empty kitchen, then returned to the second floor. "Son, you still awake?"

He heard rustling in the bed. "Daddy? What's up?"

Doug groped his way to the edge of the bed and lowered himself to the floor. He leaned against the side of the mattress, one arm resting on the cool sheet. "I just went through the papers in your backpack. I saw that your class is having a Mother's Day party later this week. How do you feel about that?"

"Gee I don't know, sad, sort of left out."

Doug's chest tightened. "I'm so sorry, son. Is there anything I can do for you, any way I can make it better?"

"Why did Mommy leave us?"

Caught off guard by the unexpected question, Doug's heart thumped painfully. His mind was immediately deluged with poignant memories from years ago. They were as real and tangible as the colorful pictures showcased in the photo album kept downstairs. Pam, dressed in frayed jeans and one of Doug's tattered t-shirts, planting a rose bush in their makeshift garden. Alex, propped in his green plastic high-chair, wearing a crown of strained carrots on his head. Samson, barely five-weeks old, a bundle of black fur chewing on a puppy toy.

The images remained fresh in his mind, crisp as a ripe red apple plucked straight from the tree.

"She never left you, please don't ever think that. She left me. It never had anything to do with you."

"But why...why did she go?"

Doug drew in a deep breath, then exhaled slowly. His chest deflated like a punctured tire. "I wish I knew. I guess she was just unhappy and --""

"But why was she so unhappy?" Alex broke in. "She had you and me and Sam."

"I know. But somehow that just wasn't enough. Sometimes people need more."

"Like what?"

It was difficult to explain to his son what he had never been able to fully explain to himself. "Oh gosh, maybe she needed to be satisfied or fulfilled in other ways. Maybe she wanted other opportunities and experiences in life. It's kind of a grown up thing. I don't know how to explain it to you."

"Were you happy, Daddy?"

"I sure was. But you see with me it never took very much. Since both my parents died when I was young, I was just so thrilled to have someone to love and a family of my own. Evidently, your mom just needed more, something I couldn't give her."

The boy rolled onto his side and yanked up the covers. "Where did she go?"

"I never knew. She just left me a letter saying she was leaving. In a couple of months, I got a notice of our divorce."

Moments later, his son asked the question he had been anticipating, truly dreading throughout the discussion. "Will she ever come back to us?"

The man considered the question long and hard before answering. He weighed what he believed to be the truth against what he thought Alex wanted to hear. Deep in his heart, he knew there was nothing to be gained by clinging to false hope. Ultimately, he said in a whisper, "No, I doubt it. I don't think we'll ever see her again."

A long silence ensued, the two wrapped in their individual reflections. As his thoughts diffused, Doug became more aware of the sounds surrounding him. The mesmerizing call of crickets outside the open bedroom window. A stray cat's haunting yowl from a nearby alley. The familiar click, click of Sam's toenails scraping the kitchen floor as he wandered about, undoubtedly in search of food.

A chill night breeze whisked through the open window and tiptoed lightly across the back of Doug's exposed neck. His drifting thoughts jerked back to the present. One final point must be made before the topic was shelved. "You do know I would have done anything to make it different for you. If I could have done something, anything at all, to make her stay in order that you'd never be hurt, you know I would have done it, right?"

The boy reached out and laid a hand on Doug's forearm. "Yes Daddy, I know."

Tears sprang into Doug's eyes at the simplicity of the answer. "I love you so much. I'm sure I have enough love for two parents."

"But what about the party?"

Doug laughed in relief. "Hey, is there any law that says a mother has to be a woman?"

"Wow, I don't know, is there?" Alex's voice was now alive with curiosity, intrigued by the novel question.

"Don't think so. Why can't I come?"

"Would you?"

"Sure, why not. You know, a guy could do worse than spend an hour around a bunch of pretty women." Doug reached over to fluff his son's hair.

"Oh Dad, most of them aren't all that pretty," Alex commented in an off-hand way before adding with a note of incredulity, "And besides, those ladies are married."

Suddenly, a sharp wind whipped through the room, the navy-and-white-striped curtain billowed wide then snapped back to the screen. The father retrieved the comforter from the foot of the bed, covered his son and tucked it around his neck and shoulders. "Who says they're all married? After all, I'm not."

"That's true," Alex conceded drowsily.

Doug rose. "Well, I better go and let you get some sleep."

The boy yawned. "So you'll be there for the party? I can tell my teacher?"

"You bet. I wouldn't miss it for anything. Doug gave the comforter one final tuck. "See you in the morning, Bud."

As he went down the stairs for the second time that evening, Doug discovered Sam poised at the front door, panting eagerly, tail wagging. "Want to go out?" In response, the lab added paw-prancing to his routine.

"Okay, okay." Doug slung on a lightweight jacket and eased the door open. Like an arrow shot from a bow, the dog bounded into the courtyard and flew around the corner to the small patch of grass fronting their condominium.

Leaving the door ajar, Doug followed at a more leisurely pace. Night sounds enveloped him as he went down the narrow sidewalk. He sat down on its concrete edge and watched Sam as he went from tree to tree, bush to bush; first sniffing to discover who had dropped by recently, then quite deliberately leaving his own calling card for future visitors. After completing his rounds, the lab loped over to Doug and flopped down, half on--half off of his lap.

"When will you ever figure out you're not a lap dog?" Ignoring the question, Sam arched his back expansively, somehow managing to ease even more of his considerable bulk onto Doug. The dog sighed in contentment, tongue lolling out the side of his mouth.

"You're hopeless," Doug concluded as he stroked the thick dark fur.

On the heels of the recent conversation, he was consumed by disparate images of his ex-wife. The conflicting thoughts were waging war against one another inside his head. There was the original Pam, his beautiful wife, the woman he had loved, shared a bed, a life and a child with. Then there was the other Pam, the woman who had promised to love him and remain with him forever, the woman who had walked out on him and injured his child.

If he saw her now, which one would she be?

Doug threw his head back and contemplated the night sky. His eyes roamed from star to star as though one might offer the solution to the various emotions rampaging through his heart and mind. But at the end of the day, they were just stars, incapable of providing anything but light and perhaps an odd sort of lonely comfort.

But he knew Pam was living somewhere under these very same stars right now. Perhaps she, too, was searching the sky, hoping for some sort of answer.

"Pam ... where are you?" He spoke the words aloud, still canvassing the sky above. The old familiar ache clawed at his heart.

At the sound of his master's voice, Sam pivoted his head. One flailing paw grazed Doug's neck, jolting the man from his reverie. Now he felt foolish at such sentimental behavior. The past was gone; all that mattered now was Alex and their life together.

"Time to go in." He gave the dog an encouraging nudge. Sam rolled off, shook, then headed for the door. Consumed only with thoughts of sleep, Doug got slowly to his feet and returned back into their home.

II

JOHN RELAXED IN HIS FAVORITE armchair, perusing the evening newspaper. From the kitchen, he heard the microwave oven sound its familiar bleat. On bare feet, he walked in and checked on his dinner through the oven's tempered glass. The telephone rang just as he was retrieving a potholder from beneath several folded dishtowels in the drawer.

In quick succession, he grabbed the portable phone, depressed the on button, shoved it between his cheek and shoulder, opened the microwave and snagged the bubbling lasagna.

"Hello." He pulled the plastic container out and gave the oven door a solid nudge with an elbow.

Although the caller offered a response, the salutation went unheard over the slamming of the microwave door. He swung around, repeated the greeting.

After a momentary pause, the still unknown caller spoke. "Johnny?"

The solitary utterance blasted into John's brain like a thunder crack. He stopped short and stood frozen in the center of the kitchen. The plastic dish clattered to the floor, striking a corner first, then flipping over onto its back like a dead bug. Steaming noodles, cheese and marinara sauce draped half-in, half-out of the container. The now-empty hand fell to John's side. The tattered green and blue checked mitt slid from his limp fingers to join the culinary carnage on the floor.

John left the kitchen, his face taking on the glazed, wide-eyed look of a sleepwalker. He lowered himself back onto the chair and opened his mouth to speak. His lips moved, but no words came out.

Instead, he was overwhelmed by memories from the past, vivid pictures shooting one-by-one through his mind like quick cuts in a film. In no time, these illustrations were augmented by other sensory memories. The pristine smell of her skin...the silky texture of her hair...the sound of her buoyant laughter.

"Johnny? Is that you?"

Blood pounded in his ears. Her voice was exactly the same-- it hadn't changed one single bit. "Yes, it's me," was all he could manage for the moment.

"Johnny, this is --"

Finally he located his voice. "I know who it is. I just can't believe it, Natalie. I just can't believe it's you."

"I bet you can't. It's been a long time."

"How did you --"

"I'm sure you're wondering --"

They both spoke at once, stopped mid-sentence. Each tittered nervously. Recovering first, he insisted, "You go ahead."

"I was just going to say, you're probably wondering how I found you."

"That's exactly what I was going to ask you."

"Well I was back in Boston about two years ago and I ran into your Mom. She told me you were living in California. She gave me your phone number."

John's eyebrows shot up in surprise. "Back in Boston? I never knew you left. Where are you now?"

"In New York, actually a little town outside the city. I've been here for about ten years."

"I guess we have an awful lot to catch up on."

"I guess we do." Diffidently, she asked, "Where do we start?"

John relaxed his death-grip on the receiver. "With you. Tell me everything."

"There's not that much to tell. After graduating from U Mass, I went to work for a large computer company in Boston, but only stayed for one year. I moved on to a smaller operation and have been with them ever since."

An unbidden memory came to John's mind of a baffled Natalie sitting paralyzed before a typewriter in a high school class. He couldn't imagine Natalie hunched over a keyboard all day. "You work with computers?" His amazement was clearly reflected in his elevated voice.

"Work with them? Me? Heck no. Believe me, some things never change. I'm in sales. And what about you? Your mother told me you had gone into some kind of social work?"

John gave a small snort. Social work, indeed. After all these years, his mother still couldn't bring herself to admit her son had joined the priesthood. Yet, as he tried to imagine telling Natalie about his chosen profession, he discovered he didn't want to do it either.

Shock ran through him like an electric charge. He had never denied his affiliation with the church. He heard himself replying, "Yeah, something like that."

Keeping his voice light, he shifted the topic back to her. "And what about the rest--did you marry, have a dozen children all shapes and sizes?"

Her answer was slow in coming. John found himself holding his breath as he waited. "No, I never married."

An absurd sense of relief swept over him. "Why not," he blurted out. The temerity of the question astonished him probably even more than it did her.

The response was instantaneous. It whipped back at him like a snapped rubber band. "Because I think you only find the right person one time. There really are no second chances in life; or at least, not for me."

John swept a hand down his face and onto his throat, acutely aware of the pulse throbbing in his neck. "Oh Natalie," he uttered.

"Johnny why did you leave me? Why did you go away and never come back?" The pain of fifteen long years punctuated every syllable.

"Didn't you get my letter?" The moment the artless query left his lips, he knew he had made a severe error. He would have given all he had to retract those words.

She sucked in her breath as pain instantly turned to anger. "Letter? Of course, I got your damn letter," she spat back at him. "So what? It was a letter, a stupid piece of paper. It wasn't you. And so you were having problems, so damn what? Couldn't we have gotten through that terrible time together and gone on and gotten married the way we had always planned? Didn't I, didn't we, deserve better than a lousy letter?" Her voice cracked, she began to cry.

"Yes, you did and we did," was all he could say. Then, for what seemed a lifetime, he simply listened to her weep. "Natalie... sweetheart." He marveled at how naturally the old term of endearment came back to him. "Please don't cry." Briefly, he considered the efficacy of a priest using such tender words with a single woman, then flung the thought aside as easily as he might swat at a gnat.

"I'm sorry; I don't think I can explain now what I was doing or thinking back then. It was such a long time ago. All I knew was I was in trouble and I didn't know how to handle it. So I did the only thing I could think of--I ran. Was it the right thing to do? No, not for me nor you. I can only tell you I was wrong."

"I know. I swear, I wasn't even going to bring up the past. I honestly thought I'd gotten over all of that years ago. Evidently, I was wrong."

A not uncomfortable silence settled around the two of them. For some time, it was enough to simply have the connection of an open phone line between them. A moment later, Natalie burst out laughing. John found himself grinning. There it was--that totally familiar sound. He would have known that laugh anywhere. Like she said, some things never changed.

"Okay, so what's so darn funny?" John demanded in mock indignation.

"I just had this flash-vision of you sitting there in some overstuffed armchair with three little kids, a Dalmatian dog and an angry wife brandishing a frying pan--all staring at you while you're trying to explain the past to some lunatic woman on the phone."

John sighed. "No, no three children or dog. No wife. Come to think of it, no frying pan."

"No? You never married, either?"

"No, never did." A lump formed in his throat. "There was never anyone else but you, either."

Silence descended once more. Finally, in a voice sounding wet with fresh tears, Natalie summed up, "Well, I think I've had about as much fun as I can take for one night. I think I'd better go. Would it be okay if I called you again sometime?"

More than anything in the world, John wanted to leap from his chair and cry yes, yes, yes. Or at the very least, he wanted to beg Natalie for her phone number, in order that he might never lose her again. He knew that was the wrong thing to do. And by even the most conservative of estimates, he'd already done enough wrong where Natalie Weaver was concerned.

John focused on subduing the note of longing that would be more than evident in his voice. In time, he managed to reply, "Sure, I'd like that."

After they exchanged good-byes, John tossed the phone onto the nearby coffee table. Then he carefully reviewed the conversation. A hundred questions roamed persistently through his mind. The most plaguing of all remained: *Why had she called? Why now?*

III

DOUG EASED THE LITTLE BLUE Toyota to the curb and switched off the engine. He turned to the lovely young woman sitting beside him. "This is it. The diamond's just on the other side of those bleachers."

Mandy Chandler climbed out of the car and the two walked through the park toward the field. The air was redolent with the fragrance of freshly mown grass. The capricious wind teased Mandy's dark hair, whipping it about like the lashing tails of a thousand cats.

"I'm so glad you could come today, Mandy. And so was Alex. He likes you."

"I like him, too." The young woman swept several long strands of hair away from her face. "Of course, that's not too difficult. He's a pretty cute kid."

"I think so, too. But then again, I'm just marginally partial."

She grinned at him. "Of course you are. You're his dad. That's your job."

Doug considered taking her hand, or perhaps placing an arm around her shoulder as they walked along. He couldn't do it. What was wrong with him? He had never, ever been shy. At this rate, the world would probably witness the second coming before he got the nerve to even kiss her.

As they closed in on the field, Mandy abruptly stopped dead in her tracks. "Sorry Doug, but I just can't stand it any longer," she blurted out.

Can't stand what? Bewildered, his mind automatically conjured a dozen different possibilities for what he might have done wrong.

"Ever since you picked me up, that's been driving me crazy." She tapped his shirt pocket with one finger. "What is that in there? It kind of looks like blood on that thing."

Still perplexed, the man looked down at his pocket, then laughed in relief. "Oh that. I forgot I even had it with me." Doug snagged one edge of the white material, then fluffed the piece of cloth out. He handed it to Mandy. She stared down at the lace-trimmed hankie with the bright red heart painted on the front.

"Mom," she read the inscription beneath the heart.

"The second-grade class had a Mother's Day party. All the kids made these for their moms. Alex made it for me." Doug cleared his throat. "I told him I would carry it to his game today for good luck."

"Bless his little heart." Mandy tucked the hankie back into the pocket and patted it gently. "Where is his mother?"

"Gone."

She touched his face with her fingertips. "Tell me about it sometime?"

The sun warmed his shoulders. The breeze fluttered through his hair. Doug felt an indescribable sense of belonging. "Yes, I will. Soon."

They turned together and went onto the field, her hand held securely in his.

"Dad, Mandy," Alex called. He streaked toward them from the pitcher's mound and skidded to a stop mere inches from their feet. Small puffs of dust and gravel showered down on their shoes.

"Hey Buddy, all warmed up and ready to go?" asked Doug.

"Sure am." Alex, cheeks stained pink with excitement, beamed at the two of them from beneath his red and white billed cap.

Mandy looked from father to son. "Can we expect a win today?"

Alex pounded one balled fist repeatedly into the worn leather of his glove as he considered. "I think so, but it's kind of hard to say. They've had a pretty good season so far."

Doug clapped his son on the back. "Well, just remember, winning isn't everything --"

Alex giggled and cut in. "I know, it's the only thing."

"You know that's not what I was going to say."

"I know, Daddy, you just want me to have fun."

Doug noticed the other uniformed kids were huddling-up. "Look, we'd better let you go. Have a good time, we'll be rooting for you." The two adults turned and headed for the splintered bleachers, where scores of parents and friends had already gathered to watch the game.

By five o'clock, the park had been vacated. The wind, though diminished, had turned chilly. The sun sank deeper and deeper into the horizon. A few sparse rays cast long shadows across the baseball diamond, making tall men out of short boys.

Doug and Mandy still perched on the edge of their seats. They cheered loudly when appropriate and groused about the judgment of the umpire when calls didn't go their way.

It was the bottom of the final inning. The opposing team was at bat; Alex's teammates were defending the field.

The next batter approached home base, tucking in the shirttail of his uniform.

Doug leaned closer to Mandy and whispered, "They put this kid in as a substitute for that other boy. I don't think we have a chance with him at bat. Aren't you just a little hard-pressed to believe he's only eight or nine years old?"

She nodded her agreement. The gold hoops dangling from her ears swayed with the emphatic movement. "I know they're making kids bigger these days, but this is ridiculous. He's a monster. They might have to start drug testing for steroids at the Little League level."

The huge boy picked up the wooden bat. He tapped his cleats with the tip, before taking a couple exaggerated practice swings. "Show off," Doug muttered.

Alex looked up at Doug and Mandy and shrugged as if to say, "What's a kid to do?"

Easing into position, Alex threw the first ball. It sailed two feet above the mud-spattered plate. The boy, displaying far more strength than skill, lunged at the ball. He managed to undercut it by at least three inches.

"That's the way," Doug shouted through scattered applause from those surrounding him.

Only a hint of a smile flirted across Alex's face as he snagged the ball from the air and prepared to pitch again. Just as before, the ball hovered directly over the plate. Except this time, the speeding bat connected with the ball dead on. The sharp crack reverberated through the stands like a pistol shot. A split-second later a second thud rang out as the whizzing ball slammed into the pitcher's forehead.

The force of the impact blasted Alex's baseball cap right off the top of his head. The hat spun wildly in the air, then plummeted straight to the ground like a wind-starved kite. The crowd uttered a collective gasp. All eyes were nailed to Alex's little face, which registered only a blank look of confused astonishment. He remained standing for only a beat, mitt dangling at one side, before teetering and collapsing to the ground.

Doug sucked in his breath, then whispered, "Oh my God." He leaped from his seat and roughly pushed others aside as he stumbled down the bleachers. He bounded across the field to where his son lay crumpled on the pitcher's mound.

Doug dropped to the ground and gathered the inert little body into his arms. "Alex," he cried. His horror intensified as he observed the ghastly bruise already emerging above the boy's left eye.

The coach, trailed by Mandy, shoved through the gathering crowd. He hunkered down alongside Doug. His face reflected the same dread carved into Doug's expression. He lifted one of Alex's limp hands. "Is your car here?"

"It's parked on the street."

"He got hit pretty hard. Better take him to the emergency room yourself. You can have him there in the time it would take an ambulance to get here."

"Right." Doug clutched Alex tight to his chest, stood and strode rapidly off the field. Mandy drove while Doug cradled Alex in the passenger seat.

"Oh Alex. You're going to be okay. You've got to be okay," Doug murmured. Tears streamed from his eyes. They splashed onto Alex's face and cut deep tracks in the dust carpeting the boy's smooth skin. "You know how much I love you, how much I need you," he murmured again and again. Doug stroked his son's hair, careful to avoid touching the swollen side of his forehead, now painted an angry purplish-pink.

They pulled into the hospital parking lot. Alex's eyelids fluttered open. For only a moment, he stared vacantly at his father. As quickly as they had opened, his eyes closed once more.

They sat in the waiting room of the Coronado hospital. "Can I call anyone for you?" Mandy clutched Alex's baseball cap. For some inexplicable reason, she had brought it along, as if his recovery was somehow tied to the little red hat.

"No, there is no one else." Doug's voice sounded as hollow and haunted as he looked.

Anguished, Mandy fidgeted on the vinyl-covered couch, rubbing her thumbs back and forth over the cap's stiff canvas material. "Can I get you anything? Coffee?"

Doug shook his head mechanically from side to side. His unblinking eyes were pinned to the swinging doors that Alex had been wheeled through a half an hour earlier. Mandy edged closer to Doug on the cushion. She draped one forearm across his back and gave his shoulder a reassuring squeeze. Although the gesture went unnoticed by him, it comforted her to touch him.

The minutes crawled by. Outside the two large picture windows, the brightly hued twilight sky slowly faded to black as the sun went to sleep behind the horizon. The coaches of both teams joined them and took up positions in armchairs on either side of Mandy and Doug.

Eventually, the doors arced open. A man in a white smock stepped out and approached the assembled group. All four stood. The doctor went straight to Doug, who impulsively reached out and grasped his forearm. "Alex, how is he? Is he going to be all right?" he fired off the questions as breathless as a man who just completed a ten-mile race.

The physician released a weary sigh. Before he could formulate a response, Doug gripped his arm tighter. "Doctor?" A manic twitch convulsing at the corner of Doug's mouth served as a visible testament to the extreme strain he was under.

"Mr. Sanders, we've done some preliminary work on your son and it doesn't look good. Although he briefly regained consciousness, he can't maintain it for any appreciable length of time. Everything indicates he needs surgery immediately."

"Then what are you waiting for? Go. Do it right now."

"I'm sorry but it's not that easy. We simply aren't equipped to undertake that type of extensive procedure here on the island.

Even if we could, our best neurosurgeon is at a conference in Pennsylvania. We feel Alex stands the best chance at Mercy Hospital."

Doug, white-faced, gaped at the other man. "Stands the best chance, you mean, of making it ... of living?"

"That's correct. We have an ambulance waiting. Mercy will contact their neurosurgeon. He is the best in the San Diego area."

"Go ahead. Do it right away," Doug instructed emphatically, then added, a fresh note of desperation rushing into his voice, "Please."

Without another word, the doctor spun around and returned to where the rest of the staff had accumulated. He issued brusque orders with the staccato rhythm of a rapid-fire machine gun. Suddenly, everyone moved, scattering in all directions like coins flung to the floor from an open hand.

Doug spoke to Mandy. "Look, I'm going directly to the hospital." He gestured with a hand to the coach standing off to one side. "I'm sure he can take you home."

She shook her head decisively. "No, I'm coming with you."

"But it might take all night."

"Fine. You find out where to meet them while I go get the car. I'll pick you up back here." She spun on a heel and walked determinedly toward the glass sliding doors, still gripping the baseball cap.

Gordon knotted the black bow tie at his throat. The telephone shrilled. He observed Alyssa rushing to pick it up. Idly, he wondered if it would be another one of "those" calls, the kind that caused his young wife to glance around furtively, then speak in hushed sexy tones, while cupping one slender hand around the mouthpiece. There were more of those lately.

Gordon elevated his chin and inspected the tie. He wondered what he should do regarding this latest marital development.

The phone slammed onto the table's glass surface. "Gordon, it's for you," Alyssa informed him, an air of irritation permeating the announcement.

He tugged the satin-edged tie until it nestled comfortably in the collar of his white tuxedo shirt. "Thanks." He walked toward Alyssa, his attention momentarily diverted by the alluring swish of black silk stockings and the heady scent of expensive French perfume.

Anger radiated from his wife. She shot him a piercing look, designed to convey her extreme dissatisfaction. "Honest to Christ, if it's that damn hospital again..."

Gordon retrieved the phone from the table and spoke into the receiver. "This is Dr. Brooks." He listened for a long time. He studied the floral pattern depicted on the Laura Ashley wallpaper and absent-mindedly traced the outline of one peach flower with a fingertip.

He nodded often. Occasionally, he interrupted to verify information or ask a pertinent question. Several minutes later, he posed the one question of greatest relevance to him personally. "Can't you get anyone else?"

He paced back and forth and listened to the expected reply. Despite the obvious futility, his mind continued to grope for other options. At once, he seized on a name and suggested, "What about Brian Hatfield? Isn't he available?"

The tenor of the reply was instantly reflected on Gordon's face, more than evident in the intensifying frown. His gut twisted as he thought about his wife. Finally accepting the inevitable, the doctor consulted his watch. He calculated the amount of time required first to deal with Alyssa, then get to the hospital.

He instructed, "Call Coronado back. Have them send him over immediately. Make sure we get all the film. Prep him the minute you get him. I'll be there in under twenty-five minutes."

He flung the phone back into its cradle and struggled to streamline his thoughts through the barrage of conflicting emotions pulsing through his mind. On the one hand, he resented the hospital's intrusion. No doubt, it would translate into another vile confrontation. Alyssa would have to attend tonight's symphony performance alone. There would be hell to pay.

Yet, on the other hand, he could already feel the familiar anticipation growing inside him. It was the desire to rush to Mercy and help that young boy. A baseball, a damn baseball had threatened this child's life? That was not acceptable.

As only a few precious moments slipped by, the second emotion--the desire to help, the need to heal--eclipsed the first. He squared his shoulders and strode down the hall to confront his wife.

IV

"FATHER LARKEN," SILVIA MARLEY GREETED with a start as the elevator doors slid open. "What a surprise to see you here so late."

John stepped out into the hall and smiled at the older woman. "I know. I was visiting someone on the oncology floor. The time just got away from me. And how about you, working the late shift?"

The nurse nodded. The braided bun crowning her head bobbed this way and that with the brisk motion. "I just came down to the cafeteria to grab a quick snack."

"I see. Well, better be on my way. Nice running into you."
He doffed an imaginary hat to her before turning toward the
hospital entrance.

He had taken only one step when Silvia lightly touched his
shoulder. "Before you go..."

"What is it?"

A shadow fell across Silvia's wrinkled face. "Just more of the
same. I shouldn't be bothering you with it."

"Hey, that's what I'm here for. That's why they pay me the
big money."

The nurse chewed the inside of her cheek. "Well, it looks as
if we're probably going to lose someone upstairs. The surgery's
been going on for the longest time. It's been touch and go all the
way. If the patient dies, I thought maybe you could be available
when we had to tell the parents."

The elevator doors began to close. John extended an arm
to prop them open. "I understand. I'd be glad to go with you."

"But it's so late."

He stepped back into the empty elevator. "Come on. You
can give me the details on the way up. "

Beneath the harsh white glare of the operating room lights,
the neurosurgeon stood absolutely still, silent as fallen snow.
Conversely, a flurry of activity went on around him. To his left,
a scrub nurse deftly removed cardiac monitor patches from the
patient's bare chest. To his right, the anesthesiologist scribbled
a few final notations in an operating room log while across the

table, an OR tech transferred used instruments onto a tray. It seemed everyone was busily doing their job -- everyone except him. He had already done his job, done it to the very best of his ability, done it until he could do it no longer. And in the end, he had failed.

Gordon ripped off the rubber gloves and flung them onto the table. The sweat-stained surgical mask that had covered his face for what seemed a thousand hours followed.

He knocked the swinging door open with the heel of one hand. He found Silvia waiting for him, a bleak expression etched into her ancient face. "Father Larken is on the floor. Shall I get him for you?"

He nodded wordlessly and she walked off down the hall. Gordon scraped a hand over the top of his head. It was an unconscious mannerism reminiscent of younger days when he had sported a thatch of thick dark hair. Now, his fingers only encountered barren scalp.

The doctor closed his burning eyes, bowed his head and pressed the palms of both hands against his face. He mentally replayed every moment of the arduous operation. Even now, he tried to think of something, anything he might have done to alter the outcome. But there was nothing. Not one single thing. Only God himself could have saved that child's life. And for some unknown reason, God had been mysteriously absent in that operating room tonight.

Gordon sensed Silvia's return. He observed the twosome standing before him. Both appeared grim. "Thanks Silvia," he said to the nurse. He opened his mouth to speak again and instantly forgot the man's name. *Jesus, he had heard it only a moment ago.*

Noticing his distress, the nurse quickly offered, "Father Larken stayed, just in case we might need him."

"I appreciate it." The two men walked together toward the waiting room.

Doug sat stoop-shouldered on the edge of the couch, with elbows resting on both knees. Mandy, one forearm flung across her face, had fallen asleep on an adjoining couch some time ago. A nurse had draped a dark brown blanket over her. The red and white baseball cap was clutched to her chest.

Doug looked up as the two men entered the small room. Funny, he'd been waiting for this very moment for hours. He had imagined it again and again in his mind. He had visualized the scene down to the very last detail. The doctor, looking the very definition of calm assurance, would stroll into the waiting room. Doug would shoot from his seat as if impelled by some huge unseen force. The doctor would carefully and quite distinctly explain that Alex was fine, had come through the surgery without a hitch. The boy would return home in just a few days. Alex would be back on the baseball mound, probably pitching a no-hitter within two weeks, no worse for wear.

Doug, heart bursting with elation, would whoop aloud in relief. He would embrace the doctor. Tears of joy would stream down his face. Mandy would wake up and join in the celebration. The trio would hug and cry and laugh for the longest time. The picture had been so real, so clear in his mind. At times, Doug thought he could actually hear their enthusiastic laughter, see the relieved smiles.

But now, Doug knew with every slow, plodding thud of his heart, the picture had been wrong, so very wrong.

The two men moved relentlessly toward Doug. He lumbered to his feet. He moved sluggishly as though in slow motion. He blinked once, twice. Through tear-swollen eyes, he gazed into the doctor's tired, ashen face.

The doctor uttered in a hushed voice, "Mr. Sanders, I'm so very sorry. We did everything we could. We were able to deal with the hematoma, but we encountered unexpected complications. The brain swelling happened too fast and far too dramatically. We tried everything. Nothing worked. Ultimately, these complications proved fatal."

Fatal, the word echoed vacantly. Doug's mind blocked reality. No, no, the doctor had it all wrong. He meant to say Alex was fine—he'd be playing baseball again, soon.

Don't you remember, Doug's heart screamed. *That's how it's supposed to go. And then we're all supposed to laugh together and be so happy.*

"Don't you remember?" Doug asked aloud in the silent room. His eyes turned glassy. All color vanished from his face. He swayed from side to side like a man who's had a dozen drinks too many. He began to hyperventilate.

The doctor and priest exchanged a knowing, worried, glance. Father Larken edged a half-step closer and placed a supportive hand beneath the man's elbow. "Mr. Sanders, I'm the hospital chaplain. Why don't we sit down here on this couch together and talk for a while."

Silvia gestured to the closed door of the operating room. "Is he going to be all right?"

John hunched his shoulders. "I really don't know. It's a lot to bear all at once."

"The poor man." She tucked a stray wisp of gray hair back beneath her bun. "And such a precious little boy. I wish he hadn't gone in there."

"I understand. But who knows what is right or wrong in a situation such as this." He gave Silvia's bony shoulder a reassuring squeeze. "Listen, why don't you go ahead. I'll wait here for him."

"Thanks. I do have a lot to take care of." She gave him an appreciative look before trudging away.

Doug stood just inside the closed door. He was oblivious to the machines and equipment inhabiting the room like mute spectators. He saw only the table. His heart and mind rebelled in unison. Each was constitutionally incapable of accepting the truth.

He took one hesitant step forward. "Alex?" The solitary utterance reverberated through the empty room. It bounced from wall to wall, floor to ceiling.

Doug shuffled over and gazed down into the face of his precious son. Alex's head was wreathed by a halo of white surgical gauze. The boy looked as if he was just sleeping peacefully. *Sleeping, only sleeping,* Doug's over-wrought mind told itself.

Weak-kneed, he hitched a hip onto the edge of the table. He was mere inches from his slumbering son. Doug picked up one of Alex's hands and held it in his own. *Cold, it was so cold.* Trancelike, Doug glanced around for his son's blue-and-white comforter. It was nowhere to be found. He frowned, perplexed. Where was it? He had always tucked it around Alex on these chilly nights.

For several long moments, he simply sat, warming the little hand between his two large ones. His unfocused eyes were fixed on some distant point, seeing nothing. Then he began to talk to his son. He spoke in a soft, yet conversational tone. "You know my mother told me a story once and I never forgot it. You never met my mother, did you?"

He stopped, waited a prolonged moment, then went on. "Anyway, it was about what babies do before they're born while they're still inside their mother's bodies. Did I tell you this, already?"

He paused again in his narrative. Doug cocked his head to one side, as if waiting for a reply. After a while, he continued, "Well, I always meant to. Anyway, she told me that before babies are born, they reach up and snatch a bit of their mother's heart and take it away with them into the world. She said that's why mothers and their children have such a deep and special bond. Yes, I always liked that story... " His voice trailed off and he began to hum a disjointed little tune of his own creation.

Suddenly, Doug flinched as if an encyclopedia had been dropped from a ledge. He lowered his gaze. Only then did he focus fully on his son. Now, he saw him clearly.

Alex was dead.

Doug drew in a ragged breath. "But the problem is, that story never explained how you managed to take all of my heart, not just a small piece. You took the entire thing." He bent over his child and clutched his narrow shoulders with trembling hands. Tears poured onto Alex's bare skin. "Don't you see," he begged. "Don't you understand, you can't leave me now. You took my heart."

Now sobbing out of control, he gathered the lifeless body up in his arms and pressed it against his chest. Immediately, he felt the obstruction. He reached down between them to eradicate it.

From his shirt pocket, Doug extracted the balled-up white hankie he had brought with him to the baseball game. The vivid red heart shone brightly in the sterile room. A wretched cry tore from Doug's throat. He flung the little hankie away as if it had literally seared his flesh. It fluttered to the floor. The "Mom" inscription landed face-up.

Doug cradled his son in his arms and pressed his wet cheek to the boy's slack face. "Alex, you've got to understand, you can't leave me now. I can't live without my heart. I cannot, cannot live without you."

V

THE BEACH WAS VACANT ON this chilly, bleak day. The only vestige of activity came from a cadre of seagulls slicing back and forth through the dank air. Their high-pitched cries reverberated through the emptiness. Occasionally, one maybe two would alight on the damp sand to investigate a patch of seaweed or plunder a bit of debris for morsels of food. Then each would take flight, provoked by some threat, real or imagined.

In time, the desolation was broken by a solitary figure ambling slowly along the shoreline. With head bowed, shoulders slumped, hands jammed into pockets, the man was a study in abject misery. His hair was disheveled. His bushy moustache was badly in need of a trim. His sallow skin was as gray as the sky above.

But it was his eyes, above all else, that spoke so poignantly of the agony contained within his heart. To look deep into those eyes was surely to see first-hand the gates of Hell.

For hours, Doug had wandered along aimlessly on the hard-packed sand, numb to his surroundings. He hadn't heard the shrill call of the airborne birds or felt the chilly water as it scampered over his bare feet, painting the bottom of his jeans a deeper blue. He simply stared blankly at the path before him. Mile after mile he walked, lulled into a near catatonic state by the hypnotic drone of the waves.

After a while, he came face-to-face with a chain-link fence. It separated the public beach from the military base. He stopped short, now forced to look up.

Immediately before him rose the dunes, the huge mountains of sand where he and Alex had so often played together. In this unguarded moment, it was almost as if he could actually see his young son. There he was, perched atop a dune. Doug heard him enthusiastically counting off the passing seconds as his father sprinted toward him.

At the recollection, a shudder catapulted through him. Doug swayed on his feet. Unimaginable pain broke through his carefully constructed defenses. He drew in a ragged gasp of air. He extended a trembling hand to the fence and laced his fingers through several diamond-shaped links for support.

A soft whimper escaped his lips. Doug dropped his gaze to the rubble strewn along the fence line. *Focus, he must focus on something else right away.* Desperate, he seized on a cigarette butt and concentrated all his attention upon it. He studied the fragments of charred white paper, the random flakes of brown tobacco spilling from the crushed tip, the pink lipstick smudge discoloring the filter. He examined it with great absorption for what seemed minutes. His heart needed time to rebuild its line of defense.

Done in by the enormous effort, he swung around and sat down heavily. Doug regarded the horizon and idly tracked the progress of boats chugging their way to distant ports. Blessedly, his mind was now void of all thought.

So consumed was he with this activity, he failed to notice the lone bird that fluttered onto the sand, less than one yard from his outstretched legs. It was a small creature with sleek lines and dark eyes.

From its vantage point on the sand, the gull regarded Doug with an even greater intensity than the man displayed for the ships. The bird scrutinized his grief-wracked facial features. After long moments, the bird seemed oddly satisfied with what it saw. It dipped its head to the moist sand and began pecking here and there for hidden booty.

It was this action, glimpsed from the corner of one eye, that caused Doug to notice the plucky little bird. His initial surprise at its close proximity, only increased as the gull, rapidly plunging its beak into the ground, moved even closer.

Only when it bumped Doug's thigh with one tucked wing, did it cease the manic pecking and stand perfectly still. It raised its feather-crested head. Without noticeable fear, it peered into Doug's face and canted its head to one side as if in question.

Doug assumed the bird would dart away in fright at the slightest movement. Slowly, he turned his hands over, palm-up. "I have no bread for you. Trust me, I'm not the one you want," he told the still motionless bird. "Alex was your friend, and he's not here." Doug sighed deeply in despair and returned to watching the boats.

Yet, when he looked back, the gull was still there. It wore the same intent expression. If anything, the bird had edged even closer toward one upturned hand. "What do you want from me?" His anguished voice was barely audible over the crashing waves.

The bird elevated its head fractionally. It stared directly into Doug's eyes with a naked, penetrating intensity. Time slowed, then stood still like a broken watch. Everything ceased to exist. All that remained was the two of them. Eyes locked together, something passed from the bird to the man. It was there, then gone. In the space of only a few seconds, a profound peace settled over his entire body. The pain, previously sizzling so hot in his heart, flickered, then died.

Doug leaned forward. "Alex?" he croaked in a hoarse whisper. "Son, is that you?"

The gull uttered a guttural sound from deep in its throat. It preened its gray and white flecked feathers and spread its wings wide. The tip of one wing lightly brushed Doug's leg. A split-second later, the bird was airborne. It executed a wide circle above the fence, then returned and hovered at a point just above Doug's feet.

The gull gave him another piercing look through jet-black eyes. A shrill cry rang through the air. The bird wheeled and flew off high above the breaking waves.

Dumbstruck, Doug watched the gull become one with the rest of the flock. In seconds they were gone, yet the tranquility bestowed upon him by this creature, remained.

VI

JOHN SLAMMED THE CAR DOOR and stepped onto the sidewalk. Raindrops, like rice thrown at a newly married couple at a traditional wedding, pelted his entire body. He studied the address posted on the side of the ivy-laden brick building, then rechecked the numbers scrawled on the scrap of paper held in one hand. This had to be it. He hustled up the walkway into the small condominium complex. Once inside the tree-lined courtyard, he located the appropriate door and knocked. Waiting, he listened to the rainwater drip, drip, drip from a dozen different leafy branches onto the sidewalk below.

Presently, the door swung open. Although the priest instantly recognized Doug Sanders, he was taken aback by the dramatic physical transformation that had occurred in such a relatively short period of time. When John had last seen him, Doug had appeared robust, healthy, an individual who took good care of himself. Now, he looked haggard, gaunt, a man far older than his years. *The tremendous price of grief,* John thought to himself as they acknowledged one-another through the dusty screen door.

"Hello Doug, remember me?" John initiated with a smile. "Father Larken, from the hospital."

The other man scowled in concentration, striving to remember. Then, the connection made, he pushed open the door. "Yes, yes I do."

John braced the screen door with one shoulder as the two shook hands. "I had to come over to Coronado today and I thought I would drop by just to see how you were doing," the priest explained, before adding somewhat diffidently, "Hope that's all right with you."

"Absolutely." Doug stepped back and motioned inside with one hand. "Please come in. It's so awful out there today."

"I agree. Definitely not our standard May weather." As he came in, the priest was greeted by a large black dog that eagerly sniffed his pants leg. "Hey there, guy." He reached down to ruffle the dog's short fur.

"Sam, leave the poor man alone."

John squatted down and scratched behind the dog's ears. The lab licked his forearm in unabashed delight. "It's all right.

I so rarely get to be around big dogs. Believe me, this is a real treat."

"Sometimes he can be a little overpowering." Doug crossed the room and gestured to a recliner. "Have a seat, Father..." He stopped short, clearly at a loss for how to address the priest.

"John," he supplied and settled into the overstuffed chair, covered in gray-blue corduroy. "Please call me John."

"Okay and before I join you, can I get you something, maybe some hot chocolate? I just got back from the beach a few minutes ago and made a cup for myself. You want some, too?"

John grinned, pleased by the offer. "I would, thank you."

Doug busied himself in the kitchen. Soon, the two sat across from one another, both holding steaming mugs.

John noticed a leather-bound photo album open on the coffee table. He referred to it with the wave of a hand. "Looking at pictures?"

Doug nodded by way of reply.

John reached over and repositioned the album to see the photos more clearly. "Halloween?"

Doug nodded a second time. "Yeah, when my son was about two."

John examined the photos. Most were of little Alex, who was outfitted in a pumpkin costume, a vivid green cap atop his head. There was an attractive woman, probably Alex's mother. Doug was there, too. Chubby-cheeked Alex appeared to be giggling with glee in every photo. The bright orange costume puffed out in all directions. The miniature green hat was always askew.

Two parents and one pumpkin, John reflected sadly to himself. Then he revised the thought to more accurately fit the current circumstance: now, one parent, no pumpkin.

The priest continued to flip pages and inspect the myriad photos. He remarked occasionally on this one or that. All the time, he considered what he could possibly say or do to help this man. Words were so inadequate in a situation such as this. And unless Doug was a believer, talk of God and His gift of salvation would be of little or no value.

John wanted so desperately to help this man. His prolonged torment had become an almost palpable thing. It was evident in every aspect of his being, from the dark hollows surrounding his haunted eyes, to the weary stoop of his shoulders.

"You know, I'm really all right," Doug suddenly offered up. He spoke as if the remark was a natural extension of a long conversation already in progress.

Startled, John closed the album and set it to one side on the wood and glass-topped table. He picked up his cup. "You are?"

"Yes, I am. Or at least, I think I'm going to be," he replied, sounding far stronger than he looked. "Something unbelievable... miraculous happened earlier today and..." Incapable of finding the right words, Doug contemplated the large, multi-paned window positioned directly behind the priest. For a long time he stared at the rain sluicing down the glass, mesmerized by the intricate designs and mosaics created by the trickling water.

In this unguarded moment, John observed an emotion flickering deep in Doug's eyes. It served as a distinct contradiction to the man's pathetic appearance, something akin to...was it peace? Intrigued, John prompted, "What was it, what happened?"

Now it was Doug's turn to appear startled, jerking slightly in his seat as if he'd somehow forgotten John altogether. Although he seemed on the verge of answering, Doug paused, as if reconsidering.

Perplexed by the hesitation, the priest urged, "Yes?"

"It's kind of a long story."

Intuitively, John knew time wasn't what lay at the root of his reticence. "There's nowhere I need to be. I have the rest of the afternoon."

Doug took a sip from his mug and looked thoughtful for some time. Finally, he spoke. "Well, ever since we moved to the island, Alex and I would take bread to the beach and feed the seagulls..." Although the words were hesitant at first, once the floodgates were open, the story poured out in a rush.

Later, the two men sat relaxed in the comfortable room. Doug snugged into the corner of the plump couch, crossed feet propped on the coffee table. John leaned back in the cozy chair, his right foot cocked on the opposing knee. With no lights burning, the room had grown as shadowy and dark as the day outside.

The empty mugs had long since been set aside. Both were silent, caught up in individual musings. Each was only vaguely aware of the drizzling rain or the occasional sighs and grunts made by Samson as he slept peacefully.

"I really believe it was God's way of telling me that Alex was all right," Doug asserted. "Do you think so?"

"Tell you what, the majority of those in the church would say you were simply seeing what you wanted to see. But I think they'd be wrong. I absolutely agree with you. I think you saw exactly what God wanted you to see." John edged forward on the cushion and anchored his laced fingers beneath his chin. "So many people just want to place God in a box. For some reason, they want to believe that He only speaks to us in certain ways, such as through the scriptures, or maybe during prayer. But I think they forget God isn't reading the same handbook, doesn't use the same scorecard we do."

The priest ran a hand through his hair in thought. "God is God. The entire world is at His disposal to communicate with. Why just think of all the ways He can show us his heart: a cloud formation, a sunbeam. In your case, a seagull. I think today the Lord gave you a priceless gift, an extraordinary gift of love. I think He wants you to know that Alex is okay. Your son is safe with Him."

Doug smoothed the edges of his mustache with the tip of one finger and nodded his agreement. The priest continued, "You know Doug, it was never God's will that Alex would leave you so soon. In this world, bad things, terrible things happen every day. But now, He wants you to know that they are together. It is an incredible blessing to have that reassurance."

Sam raised his black head, then got to his feet and loped over to the front door. Soon, a gentle rapping could be heard, barely audible over the patter of raindrops.

"Must be my day for visitors," Doug declared. He got up and went over to where Samson stood with ears perked and tail wagging in anticipation. "What a surprise," he exclaimed in astonishment. On the other side of the door was Mandy. He hadn't seen her since the memorial service.

Mandy, in jeans and a turquoise blouse with a matching jacket, looked beautiful. The damp weather had caused wisps of her long hair to curl softly around her face.

"Doug, I was baking cookies this morning and thought you might like some," she explained as he ushered her in. She noticed the other man. "Oh my goodness, you've got company. I should have called first."

"No, glad you're here," Doug said.

John got to his feet and turned to the pretty young woman. "It's Mandy, isn't it?"

She appeared mystified. A second later, she gave him a small smile of recognition. "Yes. And you're the priest I met at --"

"That's right," John cut in, wanting to negate any reference to that tragic night. "I'm John Larken. Nice to see you, again."

"Thank you." She held her plate aloft. "Can I interest you in a cookie?"

"I'd love one, but I really must be going."

"Hope I'm not running you off."

"Not at all." John went over to Doug, still standing by the open door, and shook his hand. "It was good to see you. Thank you for telling me that story. It really meant a lot to me. I will never forget it."

Doug closed the door and swung around to face Mandy. "That was nice of you to think of me while you were baking."

She gave him a crooked grin. "Actually, I sort of lied about that." Mandy broke into laughter. "Wow, in front of a priest, no less. My old grandmother would have had me on my knees repenting for days if she'd have seen that one. I probably committed some sort of mortal sin."

Doug laughed with her. It felt so good.

"The truth is, I absolutely never bake. I hate it and am no darn good at it. In fact, these stupid cookies probably taste like crap, or worse, if that's even possible. I just wanted an excuse to come over and see you. I couldn't think of anything else. "

"You didn't need an excuse."

"Well, you know how it is. It's hard to know what is right."

The two sat down on the couch. Mandy reached over and touched his forearm, then curled her fingers loosely around his wrist. "I've been thinking about you a lot lately, wondering how you're doing." Mandy repositioned her hand on his back. She gently ran it up and down his spine.

"It's been bad, far worse than anything I could ever have imagined. Especially at first. I just couldn't, wouldn't believe what had happened. I was a lot like Sam." Doug flung a hand in the dog's direction. "Poor guy. He keeps waiting for Alex to come home. For a long time, I was the same way. It just wasn't possible that he was gone."

He paused and drew in a long, shuddering breath. "Frankly, I don't know which one is worse, denial or reality. I suppose denial is a bad thing, but sometimes the truth is pretty darn hard to take."

He stopped again and hung his head like a sick animal. Mandy waited. "Yeah, I know better now, for what that's worth. I know I'm going to live through this because, I guess, people always do. There isn't a whole lot of choice. Somehow, I've just got to find a way to get along without him. Alex was my whole life, everything I lived for."

A hush settled around them, penetrated only by the whisper of Mandy's hand sliding over the fabric of Doug's shirt. After a while, he sank back into the cushions, then took her hand and held it in his. Only now did he notice how huge and luminous her dark eyes appeared in the shadowy room. "It's good to see you," he said at last. "How have you been?"

"Fine. But all of us sure do miss you down at work."

"Nice to hear."

"It's the truth. It's just not the same without you around, Doug. Any idea when you might be coming back?"

"Soon. "

"Good, I'm glad."

"There's just one thing."

Concerned by the fresh note of pain in Doug's voice, Mandy bent closer. "What is it?"

"It's just..." She gripped his hand tighter. Tears were threatening in his voice. "It's just that I haven't gone into Alex's room yet. Not once. I know I need to go through his things. I can't do it. If I don't do it soon, I probably never will."

Mandy understood. "Let's do it together."

"You and me?"

"Yes, right now."

"But, it will be..."

Impulsively, Mandy slid her hand around the back of his neck, leaned over and kissed the side of his forehead. "I know it will be hard. But if we do it together..."

That did it; the dam broke. Doug buried his face into her hair. Mandy wrapped both arms around him. She whispered tender words and stroked his hair as he cried. Occasionally kissing the top of his head, Mandy comforted him much as a mother might sooth a wounded child.

She held him tight for a long time until the tears abated. Then, in unspoken agreement, they both stood. Holding hands, Doug and Mandy went upstairs. Together, they could do this.

VII

"OKAY GOOD, THAT'S GOOD. Now give me more hair. That's right. Fluff it up. Good." The photographer called out instructions as he dipped and bobbed on the circular wall a few yards from Shea. The camera clicked. "Okay, kill the wind. Let's have makeup over here while I reload."

Two men and one woman hustled across the lush green grass. They met Shea at the edge of the fountain. She remained still with eyes closed. The men fussed with her perfectly coifed hair. The woman dusted more translucent powder along her cheeks and forehead. Additional color was painted onto her lips.

Once satisfied, they dashed back to their card table. Shea waded through the thigh-high water and returned to the statue. It rose like a Phoenix in the center of the fountain.

She sighed and hoisted herself onto its stone façade then stood waiting in her grubby cut-offs. Tepid water streamed down her long legs and puddled around her bare feet. She carefully straightened the neckline of the stunning silk blouse the client had provided for that day's shoot. The diaphanous fabric echoed the vivid green of her eyes and easily cost more money than most people made in a month.

The model propped her rear end against the statue of God only knew what and darted a glance at the horizon where the sun was finally making its getaway. "Hurry up and go away," Shea muttered to the enormous glowing orb. They would be forced to call it a day once the light failed.

Due to the schizophrenic weather and the finicky photographer, they'd been at this shoot for hours. Shea was exhausted. Her cheeks hurt from smiling. This was one of the craziest set-ups she'd ever seen. Why, they must have at least two dozen people in this park for crowd control alone. Even now, Shea could see agency employees shooing people away from the roped-off area. In their most polite voices, they encouraged spectators to return tomorrow.

Shea was baffled. Why would anyone want to come over and look at this stupid statue, anyway? She had been posing in front of it for half the day and still couldn't figure out what the heck it was supposed to be. First, she thought it was a flock of birds. Then she decided it was a bunch of waves. And now? She still didn't know and didn't care.

"Okay babe, I am digging on this light. Let's do it," Todd called as he jumped up onto the foot-high stone wall surrounding the fountain. "Now back up a little closer to those..."

Shea gave him the first genuine smile of the entire day. "Birds? Waves?"

"Whatever the frig those things are. Just throw it in reverse, okay babe?"

Shea backed as far as she dared without getting clipped by the fountain's spray.

"Wind. Give me wind," Todd shouted peevishly. He knelt down, trying to find the right angle. A young kid working at the agency during the summer months hurried over to a large electric fan. He flipped it back on and directed it toward Shea.

"Too much, turn it down," Todd barked, annoyance nearly oozing from every pore.

Clearly terrified, the intern rushed to comply. In his haste, he knocked the fan over, righted it, then fumbled with the switch.

Todd, never a living monument to patience even on the best of days, actually stamped his foot. He pointed one rigid finger at the kid. "Get off my set this minute."

The intern slunk away. Another enterprising youth sidled up to take his place and deal with the fan.

"Okay Shea, let's have it." The photographer positioned the camera in front of one eye. "Show me how much you adore this shampoo. More hair over the left shoulder. Good. That's it."

This went on for several minutes. Todd called directions while clicking photos. Shea tried to give him what he wanted. Everyone else stood at attention and held their collective breaths.

Suddenly, a man's deep voice rang out, seeming to pose a question to Shea. "Excuse me Miss. Could you possibly tell me where I might find the men's room?"

The entire set fell silent as an empty confessional. Incredulous, Todd whirled around. His eyes strafed the assembled group for the culprit just as Shea cried out in surprise, "Connor."

"Hey Todd." Connor walked up to slap hands with the photographer. He gave Shea an acknowledging wink over Todd's shoulder. "I called the agency earlier. They said you two would be out here. How's it going, man?"

The photographer sighed and shrugged far more elaborately than the situation merited. "It's going."

"I hope she isn't giving you any trouble. She really can be a pain in the ass at times." Connor jerked his head toward the statue.

Todd looked over at the model, then back to Connor. He scratched his head in confusion. "Who, Shea? No, she's good. I never have problems with her. Wish I could say the same about the rest of them."

From her elevated position, Shea observed the two men interact. She was unable to hear their conversation over the splashing water behind her. Todd, his back to her, gesticulated expansively, his hands flailing around wildly in the air. In direct opposition, Connor wore a relaxed, open expression as he gazed at Todd.

Shea and Connor had been dating for nearly two months now. This fact was as shocking to her as Connor's unexpected presence on the set today. She had never dated anyone for such an extended period of time. Trusting a man was new to her, an actual first in her life.

Now, as she looked at him, all the previous fatigue vanished in a wink. Her heart sort of fluttered in her chest. She took him in, adoring his expressive face, curly brown beard and enchanting smile. And those eyes, such a beautiful shade of blue.

Shea hooked a thumb into a belt loop on her shorts. She cocked one hip and shifted all her weight to her left leg. A little hum escaped her lips. *With those gorgeous blue eyes and her green ones, what color eyes would their children have?* The question zipped through her mind with the speed of a lightning flash. She gasped out loud in shock.

Children, what children? God almighty. Where had that come from? She was acting like some dumbstruck school girl.

Next she'd be doodling Mrs. Connor Spate on a note pad. She had definitely been in the sun too long.

"So, almost done?" asked Connor.

"Better believe it and it's only about damn time." Todd bent to retrieve the camera.

Connor took another step forward. "Hey man, mind if I take a crack at it?" He gestured toward the camera then over at Shea. "It's been months since I've worked with her."

Todd shifted his weight from foot to foot. A constellation of diverse expressions flashed across his face, everything from mild indignation to contempt. Evidently, he was trying to decide how to react to this audacious request. The silence on the set was telling in its intensity.

Eventually, Todd seemed to settle on an attitude of amused tolerance. "Sure, what the hell. Knock yourself out." He stepped down with his usual flourish and handed the camera over to the other man.

Connor thanked him and hopped onto the wall. He fiddled with the lens, then hunkered down. He moved first one way then the other, striving for the perfect angle. Unsatisfied, he stepped into the water--custom-cut trousers, leather shoes and all. He took two paces toward Shea and clicked off a few test shots. "So, we're talking shampoo here, right?"

Shea, still somewhat giddy from her recent musings, answered him. "That's right. It's a product that no woman could ever live without."

"Okay, bring your left shoulder forward and shake your head a couple of times. Perfect. The shadowing is just right. It's going to be great."

Connor lowered the camera, scrutinized the trajectory of the sun, checked the film, then turned to address the other photographer. The rest of the group had pulled tight around the fountain. "Todd, you're the best in the business and that's a fact. These days, you are, without a doubt, the Rich Gannon of commercial photography. But..." Connor's own thought drifted away as he saw the wholesale bewilderment on the other man's face. Todd's expression had reconfigured into one enormous question mark. *Briefly, Connor considered trying to explain what he meant--the NFL, the Oakland Raiders and their star quarterback—but decided to just let it go altogether.* "The point is, even though you are at the absolute top of your game, this is going to be the shot the client uses. Guaranteed."

Todd, back in his comfort zone, preened at the praise and replied, "Whatever. Fine with me. Go for it."

Connor shoved a hand in his back pocket, yanked out a leather wallet and pitched it to one of the many spectators standing on the sidelines. The crowd uttered a gasp as he stooped to one knee and was instantly submerged in water nearly up to his chest. "Okay Shea, I've just lost a lot of money on these clothes, so better make this good. Drop your chin just a little. That's it, great. Now, give me your very best smile if you want to have dinner with me tonight."

Shea smiled radiantly down at him. She gave all she had to give. He snapped off the remainder of the film, shouting encouraging words with every shot. With the final click, the sun vanished.

Connor stood straight and waded to the edge of the fountain. He tossed the camera to Todd and said, "Thanks, man."

The other photographer caught the camera nimbly with one hand. "Sure; never let it be said that Todd Max is persnickety."

Connor climbed out of the fountain, water sluicing down his pants. His leather loafers emitted squishy sounds with every step. Shea clambered down from her perch, shuffled through the water and joined him on the grass. Hand in hand, they left the set.

"Come on, just a little bite; it's so yummy," Connor coaxed and held the fork out a little farther in the air.

Shea fixed him with a determined look and raised one protesting hand. "Now, you have got to stop that! Self-control as it pertains to food is not my strong suit. If I have one bite of that cheesecake, I will be obligated to God to consume the entire thing."

"Would that be so bad? I could always order another."

"Absolutely. Every single one of those million fat grams would go directly to my thighs. There would be serious hell to pay at the agency."

Shea and Connor had just finished dinner and were relaxing at an intimate corner booth in their favorite restaurant. He was digging into a sumptuous dessert, while she lingered over a cup of black coffee. "I love your thighs," Connor declared as he rerouted the cheesecake and shoved it into his own mouth.

"Well no one else will if they get fat. So you eat the rest of that and I'll stick with this coffee. Besides, I'll need the caffeine later. I still have a lot of studying to do when I get home tonight."

Connor scrutinized her face as she raised the cup to her lips. Only now did he realize how pale and drained she looked. Or was it merely a trick of the room's meager lighting. No, come to think of it, he'd noticed her looking especially tired lately. And no wonder. Never in his life had he seen anyone work as hard as Shea; the woman was indefatigable.

A thought occurred to him. "Why are you going to school? I mean right now? Couldn't it wait? Isn't modeling full-time enough to have on your plate?"

Shea returned the cup to its saucer. "Boy, you better believe it. But modeling won't last forever. Someday, not too long from now, I'm going to be officially over the hill. And when I'm too old to sell shampoo, I want to be able to do what I've always wanted to do."

"Become an actress like every other model?"

Shea wrinkled her nose. "Don't think so; at least, not in this lifetime."

"Then what?" Connor posed the question, then sat back in his seat, prepared to wait. He'd done this dozens of times during the past couple of months. Unlike every other model in the universe, Shea was almost absurdly reticent when it came to talking about herself.

In the beginning, it had been so arduous. He would push and prod, feeling all the while like an interrogator trying to strong-arm a confession out of a criminal. But as time went on, he didn't have to work quite as hard to access personal information. Yet, he still had to wait.

Shea stared into her empty cup as if the answer was stenciled on the bottom "Well I..."

"Yes?"

"Well, I want to create a nationwide network to help children, those who are alone, abandoned or orphaned." She paused and looked over at him. He glimpsed a spark of excitement flickering in the green depths of her extraordinary eyes. "I am going to start in Southern California because that's the area I'm familiar with. Right now I am creating a team of people who are already involved in this work—kind of like a think tank. I need their input so I can get it right. I will start small, but eventually, my goal is to cover the entire country. There are so many kids in the system who need help.

Shea also sat forward and despite the dim candlelight, Connor could see animation now carved into her entire face. As if contagious, this enthusiasm radiated throughout her body. Her voice took on a new vibrancy and her lovely hands began emphasizing every word. "That's why I'm getting my degree in public administration. I need to know how to do this. I've already set up a type of foundation with my lawyers so I can funnel and invest income wisely right now. In fact, that's the only reason I agreed to do that silly sportswear line."

Thinking about it, her face and shoulders drooped in tandem as if physically weighed down by the enormity of the prospect. "Lord, I already hate those damn clothes. They're so trendy, absurdly sexy. And can we talk about over-priced. It's almost obscene. But I know women will purchase them and I will make tons of money. Someday all of the profits will translate into vastly better lives for thousands of kids..."

She talked on about her plans; her enthusiasm never waned. Wordlessly, Connor reached across the table and took her hands into both of his. Never before had he seen her so excited about anything, with the single exception of that darn cat Clyde. He could usually count on her to light up like at least a dozen Christmas trees whenever she told him one of her crazy cat stories. But now, to see her get this excited simply over the thought of dedicating practically her whole life and accumulated wealth to helping children?

It touched him deeply. Her heart was so beautiful. He felt his throat constrict and tears sting his eyes. "Oh Shea," was all he could manage as he gripped her hands tighter. It was at that precise moment, a moment he'd never forget for the rest of his life, that Connor Spate first realized he was truly and profoundly in love with Shea Lansing.

Later, outside her home, Connor and Shea sprawled in the front seat of his red convertible, held spellbound by all that nature offered up on this splendid May evening. The rhythmic song of the waves and the fragrant sea breeze were ideal adjuncts to the compelling night sky. They surveyed it together with rapt abandon.

The full moon, obvious royalty, held court above. Millions of stars surrounded this king of the night sky, silently paying homage to its undeniable majesty. Beams of light spilled from the moon like liquid silver, illuminating the entire landscape below.

Connor pointed. "Look, a falling star." A single star had separated itself from the other royal subjects and plummeted toward the earth. A barely perceptible tail of light followed the dying star along its inevitable journey. Seconds later, it blinked out, gone forever.

They returned their attention to the moon and Shea asked, "Don't you feel like it's staring at us?"

Connor rested one arm on the back of the seat and idly twirled a strand of Shea's hair around one finger. "Yep. It looks like one big giant eyeball watching every move we make. Kind of eerie. I wonder if the moon ever tells anyone about all that it sees."

"A stringer for *The Enquirer*?"

"If those fine journalists could figure out a way, I have a feeling they would slap that old moon right onto the company payroll," Connor said.

"Yep, bet they would." Shea yawned, stretched and reached for the door handle. "Guess I'm going to have to say goodnight to both of you. My books are waiting and I have the proverbial miles to go before I sleep."

"Just stay out here a little longer," he urged.

"Five minutes and that has got to be it." Shea flung one ankle onto the padded dashboard and folded her arms loosely across her chest. The green silk blouse from that day's photo shoot was long gone, replaced by casual wear, jeans and a baby blue tank top. Soon, a low giggle began deep in her throat; in no time, it erupted into full-fledged laughter. "Rich Gannon? Connor, what were you thinking? In what universe would Todd ever know anything about professional football? Designer shoes, sure, but football?"

Connor smacked a palm over his eyes. "But Gannon was the MVP; I thought everyone alive, or dead for that matter, in California knew who he was. But honest to God, how funny was that?"

"And really, whoever uses the word 'persnickety'?" Shea said through a belly laugh.

They shared the joke together for a while, then Connor drew her close and kissed her forehead. He pressed his cheek against her hair. He loved this woman. The thought drifted through his mind as smoothly as the evening breeze wafted across his skin. He liked the way the idea felt. Even more, he liked the way she felt, so soft and warm within the circle of his embrace. He loved her and wanted her. He'd never wanted a woman so much in his entire life. He had certainly never waited so long for a relationship to turn intimate.

"Shea," he spoke, his voice husky with long-suppressed desire. "I want to come in with you and stay the night."

She stiffened in his arms. His heart withered. *Damn, why had he said that? Now she'll pull away.*

As if overhearing the thought, Shea gradually extricated herself from him. She withdrew to her side of the car, placing at least a mile of emotional distance between them.

"Sorry," Connor said lamely. "I shouldn't have said that."

"Of course you should have. You have no reason to apologize. I'm the one with the problem."

"But what is the problem, Shea? Will you tell me?"

She shook her head. "I don't know if I can."

"Please try. I want to understand. Maybe I could help; maybe we can work it out together."

She offered him a thin smile. "That's all the world needs— another screwed up female story. Paging Dr. Phil. It's just one more tedious episode in the daytime TV lineup."

"No it's not. It's you," he told her, then reached over, clasped one limp hand and raised it to his lips. He kissed the tips of her fingers, then pressed them against his bearded cheek. "It's your story. That means it has value. Come on, talk to me."

It was a while before she answered. Her reply came slow and hesitant. "My real parents were so wonderful. My mother laughed all the time. She sang to me every night. She always smelled so good. My dad was a big man with an even bigger heart. Because I was an only child, the two of them spoiled me shamelessly. I loved every minute."

She faltered, gathered herself and continued. "Both of them were killed in a car accident when I was pretty young. There was no extended family to take me in."

She went on to explain how the state had no recourse other than to place her in foster homes. She bounced from one to another—no one would adopt her. Married couples only wanted infants. Finally, a childless couple agreed. Shortly after the adoption, the wife, as sometimes happened in these cases, became pregnant.

Shea hung her head and bit a thumbnail. She swept her hair back over her shoulder with the other hand and elaborated in a voice that was barely audible. "They got their baby. Jill was the child they had wanted for so long. I was just baggage, an interloper they'd never truly wanted in the first place. I swear, if they could have returned me, like a defective vacuum cleaner, they would have."

"All those years, if a family outing was planned, like a movie or special dinner at a restaurant, it was scheduled when I was working. I always had part-time jobs after school. At Christmas, they didn't even bother with nametags on presents. The big, pretty gifts were always for Jill. Seriously, it would be laughable if it wasn't so damn predictable and pathetic. Don't even get me started on Valentine's Day or Easter. Huge red hearts and chocolates, giant baskets and stuffed rabbits for my sister; there might have been a token cup of those chalky hearts with the silly sayings or jelly beans for me, but that was about it. It was painfully obvious: I was not theirs."

Connor snaked a hand around the back of her neck and squeezed one slender shoulder. Beneath his grip, he could feel her body tremble with emotion. She inhaled, exhaled, and then repeated, "I was not theirs. That changed everything."

Composing herself, she drew her thighs up to her chest, wrapped her arms around her legs, and rested one cheek on her knees. Huddled there, she looked like a whipped dog, as forlorn and dejected as she sounded.

Connor considered what she had told him. Growing up unloved was surely an awful thing, especially after experiencing what true parental love felt like. But intuitively, with every fiber of his being, he knew there was more. "Shea," he ventured, giving her a verbal nudge, "Did anything else happen? Is there more to this story?"

She turned to face him. In the frosty moonlight, he could see tears brimming in her eyes. He had never seen her cry before. "Connor, you don't want to hear this."

He swallowed hard. Shea was right. He didn't want to hear it. But wanting and needing were opposite sides of the same coin. "Yes, I do. Please tell me."

"But I never..."

"I know. But it's time."

Seconds went by. She gazed up at the heavens. "My bedroom was a converted single car garage. It had a little tiny bathroom. Jill's room was next to the master bedroom, which made sense. They wanted her close to them."

Her shoulders lifted, fell. "I started modeling in high school. A two-bit agency was looking for local talent. They selected me and I started doing some work for them. A nationwide firm in San Diego saw my work and signed me. The money I brought in during the following years not only took care of all the family bills, but paid for several vacations for them as well as private school for Jill."

Connor knew she had intentionally gone off on a bunny trail about her modeling in an effort to avoid the unavoidable. Although he understood and respected the obfuscation, he gently moved her back to the topic. "And what else?"

She shifted in her seat. "It was right before high school graduation. I was moving out soon, so I was in the process of taking down a poster of some boy band that I worshipped at the time. I looked up and saw something odd. Once I realized it was a tiny camera, cleverly hidden in the molding, I did a thorough search. Another one was tucked into a bathroom light fixture."

She gave a small whimper; her breathing grew irregular. "The upshot to this story is that my 'father' had been spying on me, videotaping and taking still photos of me for years. I had always thought the man was a pervert by the way he looked at me, but since he had never actually touched me, I thought I was safe. I was wrong."

A low animal sound, a type of growl, emanated from her throat. Clearly, this recollection, this confession, was exacting a tremendous toll. "A bedroom, and especially a girl's bathroom, is such a vulnerable, private place. Oh Connor, you just don't know. I went from being a girl to being a woman in those rooms—that covers a lot of territory. It was so humiliating." Her respiration escalated. "The thought that he watched it all made me feel dirty, so dirty, embarrassed and ashamed..." Shea's voice slowly disintegrated into nothingness.

Staggered by what he had just heard, Connor's hands curled into angry fists. The muscles in his jaw tightened to stone. His cheek twitched. Her infinite anguish was nearly palpable, an actual force, inhabiting the space between them. Chewing glass would have proved less painful than digesting what she just told him. Shea's step-father, violating her in such a disgusting manner. That twisted, sick fuck undoubtedly jerked off looking at pictures or videos of her. If he was here right now, Connor would kill him.

Determined to leave nothing out, Shea summed up, her voice tight and hoarse, "I confronted him with it. He didn't even try to deny it. I made him give me everything. I told him in no uncertain terms that if I ever saw a single photo of me from when I was young show up in the media, I would sue his ass into the next dimension. Worse, I would tell Jill, his beloved daughter, what he had done to me. My step-mother was there. I could tell she knew about it all along.

"I looked at some of his collection, but not all. I wasn't strong enough. In the end, I destroyed everything. And yet, I still have nightmares that, one day, leftover pictures, something he might have held back as a 'special' souvenir, might surface and some filthy tabloid will expose and exploit me again. I am always so afraid."

Shea bent forward, hands clamped on the dashboard. Her tortured breathing moved from ragged shallow intakes of air to full-fledged hyperventilation.

It was terrible to watch, even harder to listen to. Every wracking gasp contained a sound of pure torment. If misery, augmented by retroactive shame, grief, and anger, had a sound, this was it. Grimacing, he placed his palms on both sides of her rib cage and pressed in, trying to calm her. Her body was overheated, quaking with every breath. He moved his hands up to grasp her shoulders. "Oh baby, I'm so sorry. It's okay," he said again and again, though he knew it wasn't. When the worst of it appeared to be over, he eased her back into his arms and held her close. Shea crumpled into his body as though she possessed no bones. Intermittent shudders flashed through her, but these too abated in time.

Connor's attention was caught by the sound of a rumbling engine. A commercial jet, not two-hundred yards away, streaked through the star-speckled sky, briefly bisecting the moon. Wing lights flashing, landing gear down, the airplane rapidly closed the distance between itself and the San Diego airport. Narrowing his eyes, Connor could just make out passenger faces framed in the tiny windows. How many of those people had also endured abuse in their lives? Such trauma was so pervasive.

Throughout his tenure in the fashion industry, Connor had certainly heard his fair share of horror stories from models. Each was unique, showcasing various forms of emotional, physical, or sexual abuse. But they all had one thing in common: men. Men perpetrated the violence, women served as their victims. And nine out of ten times, for some arcane reason, it was the woman who bore the shame and guilt of the act. Why? Connor wished he understood this dynamic, because right now he was holding this precious creature, the woman he loved, and he had absolutely no idea what to do or say. Killing that son-of-a-bitch would have been so much easier.

"Sweetheart, I am so sorry, so damn sorry that he, that both of them, hurt you. I love you. I promise, no one will ever hurt ou again. I will never let that happen." He clutched her tighter, ssed her temple. "I love you so much, Shea."

In the next instant, she craned her neck and stared up into his face. Genuine astonishment was now etched into her expression. "You do? You love...me?"

"Yes, I do. I love you completely, with all my heart."

The look of vast incomprehension remained chiseled on her exquisite features. "But why, why would you?"

As if a thousand-watt light bulb had literally sprung to life above Connor's head, comprehension struck. Shea's parents, though not intentionally, had abandoned her; the adopted parents had never loved her, only valued her for the money she brought in. All the while, her step-father was involved in unspeakable activities that reduced Shea to a mere object for his sexual amusement and gratification. In order never to be hurt again, she erected a sky-high emotional wall that even Conner had difficulty scaling.

His deep despair at the utter wrongness of her life was rapidly eclipsed by a real sense of hope. Because that was then, and this was now. Because, by God, he was going to systematically tear that wall down and it was going to start right now.

His muscles relaxed as he cuddled Shea. "Baby, I know you said you had studying to do tonight, but that's just too damn bad. We have better things to do," he explained, a low chuckle underscoring his words. "And you have only yourself to blame for this, young lady. You were the one who asked the question in the first place."

"What question?" He could barely hear her through the thick fabric of his shirt.

"I believe it had something to do with why I would possibly love you. So, now I plan on answering it. This may take hours."

Tucked away in Connor's car, the two discussed the importance of perception versus reality, the past versus the present. He spoke of his love for her, the many reasons for it, and what he hoped the future might hold. Recognizing this would be only one of many conversations, he addressed the concept of personal culpability. Shea's step-father was the guilty party, not her. He knew it would take time to chip away those feelings of personal shame, but they could do it together. They had the rest of their lives.

The earth turned, the stars and planets shifted position in the sky. Connor and Shea talked long into the night; and from its exalted throne in the sky, the moon just watched...and it never told a single soul about what it saw.

PART
IV

July, 2002

I

THE LA JOLLA HYATT COCKTAIL lounge was identical to a thousand other California bars. A stool-lined mahogany bar boasted gleaming brass accents. A smattering of intimate booths lined two walls. A handful of small tables dotted the carpeted floor. Recessed lighting, augmented by soft music, sustained a subdued atmosphere. Cigarette smoke, cloying as cheap perfume, hung suspended over the bar like a gray canopy.

On this July evening, the room was inhabited by six people: five patrons and one bartender. A man and a woman, speaking in low tones, perched on barstools. Two salesmen chugged beer in a booth. A young woman sat alone at a corner table, nursing a cocktail.

She had a beautiful face framed by abundant blonde hair and wore a glittery teal dress, as tight as it was short. Matching stockings completed the look. This striking creature was the topic of much of the beer-drinkers overt attention, taking the form of grins and winks cast in her direction. The fact that this flirtation was in no way reciprocated seemed to trouble them not in the least.

"Yo, beer tender," one salesman hailed drunkenly.

The middle-aged man replaced the glass he was polishing on the counter, draped the monogrammed dish towel over one forearm and ambled across the carpeted floor to the booth. He conversed briefly with the salesman, then went back and began mixing a drink behind the bar.

"Miss? This is for you," the bartender announced moments later to the woman.

Arching an eyebrow, Alyssa Brooks offered him a questioning look as he placed the cocktail before her. "Scotch rocks, compliments of the two gentlemen in the booth."

"But I really don't want it."

"Well, I'll just leave it here. It's a double—the good stuff. And hey, it's paid for." He stood straight, his back to the two men and dusted his hands together. "Listen," he spoke in a conspiratorial voice, "I've watched these guys in here the last couple of nights. They're part of that small appliances convention in town. Just want you to know, they're harmless. They're so gassed up right now, I give them about five more minutes before both of them pass out, and I got to call the desk so security can haul them back to their rooms."

Alyssa gave the bartender an appreciative smile before he walked away. She picked up the Scotch she was currently working on and took a generous swallow. Her thoughts automatically returned to her precious Nick. He was so extraordinary, the most breathtaking man she had ever seen. She imagined him as she had seen him thirty minutes earlier in their usual room on the tenth floor: stretched out naked on the king-sized bed, both hands folded behind his head, his dark penetrating eyes raking her equally naked flesh.

Alyssa made a soft sound deep in her throat. He was the most skilled lover she had ever been with. The sex was nothing short of mind-bending. He did things to her that most women just read about in books. Nick was every man she had ever known and a hundred men she had only dreamt about all rolled into one. He was the real deal.

Contemplation of Nick caused her pulse to quicken as heat oozed through her body. She uncrossed and recrossed her legs. Alyssa drained the last of her Scotch and replaced the squat glass on the table. In an effort to distract herself, she considered the future. How long would it be until they could be together forever? She mentally calculated the vast sums of money she had already accumulated.

From the moment she had married Gordon, Alyssa had squirreled money away in private bank accounts. A little here, a little there. She had never expected the marriage to last more than a year. So, she diligently saved for the day when she would be single once more. No more cocktail waitressing or temp work for this girl.

Surprisingly, she had remained in the marriage far longer than originally anticipated. And why not? Gordon was so easily manipulated and non-demanding. She adored her La Jolla home and pampered lifestyle. When boredom set in, there were always men, so many other men to help break the monotony.

Alyssa consulted her diamond and sapphire wristwatch, a gift she had bought herself on her last birthday. She picked up the fresh drink. *Might as well enjoy it. There was nothing waiting for her at home and she did love good Scotch. She darted a glance over at the salesmen; naturally, they were staring right at her. When it came to men, Alyssa had never doubted her own power. Knowing the gesture would drive them crazy with lust, she licked her lower lip lasciviously with the tip of her tongue. Their eyes bulged. Toying with men was one of her favorite pastimes—they were all such simple creatures, so predictable and so damn easy.*

II

"GOODNIGHT, BILL, DRIVE CAREFULLY," Gordon called one final time before closing the front door. He returned to his study and drifted over to the French doors, thrown wide to welcome the cool evening breeze. He watched Bill Emmerson, his closest friend for more than three decades, climb into his forest-green Cadillac, gun the motor, then back out of the long driveway.

Gordon drew in a deep breath of the fresh air and stretched widely, extending both arms above his head like a "V." Familiar night sounds, the chirp, buzz and hum of insects residing in the garden, surrounded him. In the spill of light from an outdoor lamp, moths practiced their relentless, hopeless dance of desire. The silver-white moon hung huge and heavy in the dark sky. Still yawning, he crossed the tile floor and reclaimed the beige leather easy chair he had vacated only moments earlier, propping his feet on the adjoining ottoman. He retrieved the brandy snifter from the side table and regarded the companion chair positioned on the opposite side of the stone fireplace. The compacted leather seat cushion still bore silent witness to the hours it had endured Bill's considerable weight.

Gordon, relaxed and content, slouched in the cozy armchair and sipped the Courvoisier. He savored the rich flavor as it tickled his nose. He couldn't remember the last time he had laughed so hard and enjoyed an evening so very much. What crazy stories he and Bill had told one another, rehashing experiences as far back as college, medical school and the early years of private practice.

Gordon recalled the best story of the lot, the one involving the misplaced cadaver. He threw his head back and hooted out loud in the empty room. He chuckled to himself for several minutes, picturing his friend's exaggerated gestures and screwed up facial features as he had recounted the details. Gordon had heard the outrageous tale at least a half-dozen times before; and of course, Bill had embellished it shamelessly.

Gordon wiped his streaming eyes and observed two brilliant beams of light strafing the wood-paneled study wall. Alyssa was home. His jovial mood vanished. How unfortunate. The thought of his wife returning home should complement his happy mood, not destroy it.

His eyebrows pinched together in a frown as he cocked an ear, listening. Alyssa, never a sedate driver at the best of times, was streaking up the driveway, speeding toward the garage. Gravel pinged loudly in the wheel wells of her Mercedes.

Moments later, he heard the back door slam shut, followed by the familiar clacks of Alyssa's high heels striking the Mexican tile floor. "Gordon," she shrieked. "Gordon, where are you?"

Alarmed, he scrambled to his feet and started for the hall, calling back, "In here."

In the doorway, he caught sight of her running down the hall toward him. He barely had time to take in the sexy green dress his wife was wearing before she threw herself into his arms. She was sobbing in near hysteria. "Gordon, please help me."

Although concern catapulted through him, all he could really take in was how good it felt to have a woman's arms around him. He savored the feeling for only a short time, before taking action. He placed both hands on her narrow shoulders and eased her back. "Alyssa, what's happened? What's wrong?"

No answer was forthcoming. Instead, her makeup-smeared eyes swung wildly around. They darted this way and that as though tracking the flight of a high-speed insect.

"Alyssa," Gordon repeated. He gave her shoulders a gentle shake. "Alyssa, tell me what's going on."

Eventually, she seemed to gain a modicum of self-control. "Oh God, it was awful. I was driving home along High Street. I had just left The Blue Spruce, where, where Sandra and I were having drinks. Remember I told you I was meeting her there tonight? Or maybe I forgot. That's not important.

"So I was driving home on High Street. I guess I wasn't paying enough attention and, and --" her babbling abruptly ceased. Her eyes began that peculiar manic searching once more as if looking hard for something.

Gordon, frustrated by the strange behavior and disjointed explanation, shook her again. "And what?"

Her huge terrified eyes snapped back to his. "I was speeding, yes, that's it. I was speeding and the cops saw me and..." A fresh flood of tears burst from her reddened eyes. She stammered out the remainder of the reply, her normally husky voice now thin, high-pitched. "They followed me all the way home. And, and if they get me, they'll take my license away. Remember they told me that the last time I got pulled over for speeding? Oh, Gordon." Breathless, she fell against him once more, her arms wrapped around him in a cleaving embrace, her chest heaving against his.

He patted her back. The combined aromas of perfume and Scotch wafted up to inflame his nose. Her body felt warm pressed up against him. He could have stood there forever.

Abruptly, she pulled away and hurdled forward with her monologue. "Tell them it was you driving the car tonight." She whispered as if afraid someone might hear her in the next room.

Gordon gaped at his wife in disbelief. "What?"

Alyssa grabbed the front of his shirt with one perfectly manicured hand. She tugged on the fabric. Her ravaged face registered optimism. "Tell them it was you driving the car. I'm sure they didn't actually see me. Besides they'll believe you -- everyone believes doctors."

"But," he tried to interject.

"You have a perfect driving record. They'll probably let you off with a warning. Oh, Gordon, please do this for me, please, honey just this once." She flung both arms around his neck, flattened her body against his and kept pleading, "Please, Gordon, I know I haven't always been the best wife, but I'll try harder. Really, I will. Help me just this one time, please."

Alyssa blathered on and on. Gordon, unaware of his own state of inebriation, was dumbfounded. His thoughts were disjointed, confused. The only thing he was truly sure of was how good Alyssa felt.

He absently stroked her soft blonde hair and considered the situation. So Alyssa had been speeding. All in all, not such a big deal. And what if he claimed it had been him behind the wheel... what was the worst that could happen? Perhaps a ticket or just a warning. And maybe if he helped her in this way, maybe things between them might improve. It felt so remarkably good to be needed by his wife.

They heard the crunch of gravel in the driveway simultaneously. Alyssa lurched back and asked, "Will you do it?"

"Sure, I will."

She gave him another quick hug. "Thank you, Gordon. Thank you so much." She bent over to snatch her handbag from where it had fallen to the floor, then bolted down the hall toward their bedroom.

A minute later, the doorbell chimed. Although expected, the sound was nevertheless, startling. Could the police really be at the front door? This situation was surreal. Gordon shook his head in an effort to clear his muddled mind, then ambled toward the door, taking a moment at the hall mirror to check his appearance. He straightened his shirt and dusted off a small makeup smudge marring the dark material. Gordon gripped the knob and pulled the door open as the bell clanged a second time. Two uniformed men, both with stocky builds, stood on the flagstone stoop. One was clean-shaven, while the other sported a well-trimmed moustache.

"Good evening, officers," Gordon greeted in an affable voice, striving to sound natural. "Is there something I can do for you?"

The mustachioed man stepped forward and elucidated. "Yes, we think so. I'm Officer Brown and this is Officer Tugman." He scrutinized a clipboard held in one hand, then flipped a couple of pages in search of information. "Are you Mr. Brooks?"

"Dr. Brooks," Gordon amended. "Do I know you?"

Brown, wearing a solemn expression, shook his head. "No, Doctor, we got your name through the DMV. Are you related to Alyssa Brooks?"

"She's my wife."

"Is she currently at home?"

Gordon nodded in reply.

"Can we please step inside?"

"Certainly." Gordon edged the door back and the two men entered the house. "Now, what is this all about?"

The question went unanswered. "Did your wife just return home a couple of minutes ago?"

Gordon hunched one shoulder and spread his open palms out wide. "I don't know. I just got home myself."

The men exchanged a significant look. Brown rubbed his nose thoughtfully. "Who drives the yellow Mercedes?"

"Why that's my car," another voice chimed in. All three sets of eyes swung around to observe Alyssa coming down the hall. The surprise Gordon initially felt was trumped by pure stupefaction when he saw what she was wearing. It was the pink flowered robe with the white terrycloth lining he'd given her last Christmas; the one she had refused to wear, scornfully labeling it sexless and matronly. The sexy cocktail dress must be concealed beneath the cotton fabric. All the smeared makeup of moments earlier had been scrubbed clean. Her hair was combed.

Caught in the soft glow from the foyer light, his wife looked fresh, attractive and impossibly young. Gordon was painfully aware of how strikingly dissimilar their ages must seem to these two strangers. He could almost hear their brains whirring, rushing to calculate the huge age differential between the old guy and this pretty young thing.

Alyssa sidled up alongside Gordon, insinuated an arm around his waist, then demurely addressed the officers. "Yes, that little yellow car is mine. You're probably here about the tags or something else I undoubtedly forgot to do."

She paused, leaned her head against Gordon's chest and glanced up at him, her face a study in wifely adoration. "Well, I guess you'll just have to discuss such matters with my husband. He handles everything around here. But before I leave you men to business, do either of you officers want anything? I could brew a pot of coffee?"

Both declined the offer with appreciative smiles. Alyssa turned to leave. "All right, I guess I'll just be forced to go back and finish my book." She retrieved a paperback novel from a front pocket. "I've been engrossed in this story all evening. Can't wait to see how it ends."

If Gordon hadn't witnessed the Oscar-worthy performance himself, he would not have believed it. The doctor had never seen anything like that before in his entire life.

The officers turned to face him once again. "So you're the one driving the Mercedes on High Street tonight?" the clean-shaven man asked, speaking for the first time. Now, his voice was belligerent and angry, his eyes cold.

"Yes, that was me."

"Didn't you just happen to notice the police car following you?"

"Listen," Gordon began, confident, congenial. "I'm sure I know what this is all about. I know I was speeding tonight and --"

The officer gave a derisive grunt, repeated the word in a questioning tone. "Speeding? You better damn well believe it. We clocked you at eighty-five."

Gordon's eyebrows shot up, aghast by the revelation. How had Alyssa achieved such a high rate of speed on such a tranquil suburban street? A light film of sweat broke out on Gordon's brow, his hands grew clammy. "Really, I honestly had no idea I was going that fast. But I'm sure we can work something out."

Tugman sighed in obvious disgust. He shook his head with slow deliberation and folded both arms across his chest. His next statement came at Gordon like an advancing army equipped with deadly firearms. "Uh-huh, and now you're going to tell me you had absolutely no idea that you ran down that poor old man walking his dog?" He paused, allowing his words to sink in, taking a moment to reload. "Well, since you appear to be fresh out of ideas, allow me to fill you in. We contacted the hospital just before pulling into your driveway and learned he was DOA."

Everything stopped. Silence inhabited the space like an uninvited, unwelcome guest. The two men stared at Gordon; he stared back. A clock ticked in a nearby room.

Then, the officer began enumerating the charges on his fingers. "So doc, looks as if we've got you for DWI, hit and run and vehicular manslaughter at the very least. I have no doubt a blood test will confirm the first while the damaged front fender of that sharp little sports car will probably verify the rest."

Light-headed, Gordon swayed on his feet. Brown stepped forward and removed a laminated card from the breast pocket of his khaki-colored shirt. Before he began reading, Tugman clucked his tongue, then offered one final off-hand remark, "Incidentally, Doctor, just in case you're keeping score, you killed the dog, too."

"Gordon Brooks, you're under arrest. You have the right to remain silent..." The carefully enunciated words slowly faded away into an unrecognizable drone. Gordon's stunned eyes swept down the long hall, eventually coming to rest on his and Alyssa's bedroom door. It remained solidly and securely shut.

III

RICHARD HAPSBURG PREENED BEFORE THE wide mirror in the doctors' locker room of Mercy hospital. He turned this way and that, appraising his image. He smoothed the lapels of the expertly cut tan and navy pinstriped jacket and flicked an invisible speck of lint from the left elbow. He stepped back to examine the knife-sharp pleats in the matching pants. The new Italian suit looked better than expected. And with any luck, it would look even more at home draped across a hotel room chair in less than two hours time.

The doctor grinned at his reflection. Yes, it promised to be a red-letter day. The early-morning surgery had wrapped up faster than expected, allotting more than ample time to shower and dress for the important rendezvous ahead.

He pictured his lunch and soon-to-be bed partner, the sexy new floor nurse in the trauma unit. He imagined her magnificent breasts teasing the skin of his face, her long blond hair whispering across his abdomen, her full lips wrapping around his throbbing...

The door burst open, whacking against the wall, and another doctor strode into the room. The erotic vision instantly withered. Richard nodded a perfunctory hello to his colleague, grabbed his briefcase and walked out.

As he strutted down the hall toward the elevator, his thoughts shot back to Gordon Brooks. Throughout the morning, while monotonously bagging the patient, Richard had thought of little else. The arrest had been all the buzz on the hospital grapevine that morning. Yet, try as he might, Richard could find no trace of the scandal in the daily newspaper.

Richard had longed to revel in graphic coverage, splashy headlines, perhaps even photos of that bastard in handcuffs, doing the perp walk. Instead, what had he gotten from the San Diego Union/Tribune? Dick. No story, no pictures. His smile reconfigured into a furious frown. His face carried this expression all the way to his car, parked in the doctor's lot. He climbed in. *By God, he was going to get to the bottom of this.*

He swung the gold Lexus into the brilliant July sunshine and onto the busy street. Simultaneously, he whipped out his cell phone and speed-dialed the number of a friend at the paper.

"City desk, Wexner."

"Ira, it's Richard."

"Hey, how the hell are you? I haven't talked to you in a coon's age."

The anesthesiologist clamped the phone tighter to his ear, straining to hear over the muffled sounds of street traffic and the blowing air conditioner inside the car. "Yeah, I've been real busy. Listen, I'm calling about a story. Do you know anything about this local doctor who was arrested last night in some sort of hit and run situation?"

"Sure, of course. It's all we talked about in the morning meeting."

"Well, why wasn't it in your paper today?"

"It was a no can do. The story came in way after deadline for the first edition. But we'll get it in tomorrow. McBride from the police beat is on it."

At a red light, Richard digested what he'd just been told. He tapped on the padded steering wheel with an index finger as his eyes narrowed in concentration. An intriguing idea, one with definite possibilities, took root in his mind. He had waited a long time, months in fact, to exact revenge on that prick Gordon Brooks. Now, the revenge was going to be bigger and sweeter than ever thought possible.

The light changed to green and Richard nosed the car forward. "Is this McBride there? I'd like to talk to him."

"Yeah, I see him on the other side of the newsroom." Ira hesitated. "Hey, what's this all about?"

Richard realized he must exercise a certain degree of caution with his friend. He cleared his throat. "I happen to know a lot about this particular surgeon. I thought I might be able to help you guys out a little with the story. You know, like... background."

"We journalists are always in the market for new sources," Ira confirmed. "I'll connect you with him right now. "

After only a moment, Richard heard, "McBride."

"Yes, this is Dr. Richard Hapsburg from Mercy hospital."

The man exhaled loudly, an obvious affectation used to convey extreme irritation. "Listen, I'm late for an interview on the other side of town. I really got to hit it. Can you make this fast?"

Richard bristled at the reporter's arrogance and combative manner. He glanced over at the young woman in the next car. *Great tits*, he decided as he inspected her cleavage. He licked his lips and flashed a salacious grin. She looked away. "Bitch," he muttered under his breath, slamming the accelerator to the floor.

"I understand you're working on the Brooks story, the doctor who got nailed last night?" He eased the car into a vacant parking space in front of the French bistro where he would soon meet the nurse. He put down the window, switched off the engine.

"Yeah, what about it?"

"I've known and worked with this doctor for a long time. I might have some additional information about him for your story that you probably won't be able to get anywhere else." Richard flipped down the visor to thwart the afternoon sun. "But I want it understood my name doesn't appear anywhere in the story. This is totally off the record. You can refer to me as a source, that's it. Got that?"

Richard pursed his lips and waited while this intellectual kingpin took the time required to synthesize such complex information. Extending one hand, splaying the fingers wide, he examined the result of his most recent manicure. The clear polish was a nice touch. The gold of his wedding ring glinted in the sunlight.

Finally, the reporter asked, "Why the need for anonymity?"

Richard smirked. The guy was hooked. "Once I tell you the things I know, you'll understand."

"Okay, I'm in," McBride agreed. The initial taciturnity was gone, the important interview now forgotten. "Go ahead; tell me what you know about our good doctor."

Richard settled back, flung his right leg across the empty passenger seat. He took only a moment to consider just how much he could say without exceeding the realm of believability. He began to talk. Relishing the power, he created the most believable of lies, each guaranteed to whet the appetites of the most jaded of readers. And as the minutes slid by, his victorious smile only grew more triumphant with each damaging, deceitful word.

IV

DOUG SIGNED, THEN DATED THE bottom of the document. He laid it on top of a tall stack of papers accumulating on one corner of his desk at work. He clicked the ballpoint pen closed and tossed it onto the blotter. Doug glanced at Alex's second-grade class picture propped alongside the black phone. Although a couple of months had passed, he found that the grief he felt looking at his son never diminished.

Although he truly believed Alex was safe with God, he just could not reconcile the "why" of his son's death. *Why did he die? People receive head injuries every day and survive. Why didn't Alex?*

To divert his attention, he picked up his empty mug and wandered into an adjoining alcove. He headed for the coffee maker and observed Vic sitting behind the front counter, nose buried in the morning newspaper. "Hey, I didn't know you were here."

"Yeah, snuck in early." His friend never lowered the Union/Tribune. "Thought I'd come in and read the paper, then catch up on a few things before the day officially begins."

"Sounds familiar." Doug filled his mug then busied himself with sugar and powdered creamer, all movements measured and deliberate.

Doug heard Vic mutter under his breath, "Holy shit." Puzzled, Doug stopped short and watched as the man flung the San Diego newspaper down onto his lap, then continued to read.

"What is it?" asked Doug, concerned.

His colleague looked up, face as gray as the newsprint. "Alex's doctor, the one who operated on him. What was his name?"

"Brooks, Gordon Brooks." Fear nibbled at the base of Doug's spine. "Why do you ask?"

"That's what I thought."

Doug, dread intensifying, crossed the floor and snatched up the paper. The bold headline leaped from the page and poised itself like a razor-sharp knife at the edge of his heart. "Drunk Doctor Implicated In Hit & Run Homicide"

Thirty minutes later, Doug was back in his office, the newspaper spread out across the desk in front of him. He had read, then reread the article at least a half-dozen times. And with every reading, he felt the poison-tipped knife plunge deeper into his heart. Now, he sat still, eyes nailed to the text, key words and phrases about the arrest leaping out at him. Alcohol-level. Elderly man. Bloody paw prints at the scene of the crime. Vehicular homicide.

Additional items concerning the suspect jumped from the page. Possible drug usage. Performing surgery while intoxicated. Nurses allegedly refusing to work with drunk physician.

His breathing grew labored, his eyes lost focus. He felt the knife cut his heart out completely as one after another, the implications struck him.

At once, the dark black type on the page vanished, replaced by recollections from the night of Alex's accident. In his mind, Doug could see the nurse, actually hear her voice as clearly as if she were standing a foot away. "We reached the doctor just as he was leaving for a night out on the town." Then hours later, after the surgery, there was additional evidence. The doctor's bloodshot eyes. The sickly pallor of his skin. The noticeable tremor in his hands as he spoke.

Night on the town. The words hammered relentlessly in Doug's mind. Had Brooks been drinking? Using drugs? Before operating on his son?

The man's unrestrained thoughts took flight and darted out of control in every direction. They collided into one another in an effort to create a new, more reasonable, scenario, and finally, somehow make sense of Alex's tragic death.

For long moments, distorted images flashed before his mind's eye. Eventually, the disjointed fragments melded together, crystallizing into one cohesive vignette: Brooks, impaired, hovering over the table, cutting deep into Alex's defenseless head. Nurses, unable to intercede, watch helplessly. The scalpel slips, slicing into the exposed brain. The machines go flat. A cover-up is established. Everyone enters into a conspiracy of silence to protect the doctor and keep the hospital safe from recrimination.

Doug knew his son should never have died. Now, he could see it so clearly. He replayed the scenario again and again, until the truth inevitably eroded away and the past was rewritten. In the space of a few seconds, a fresh scenario was born. A benign baseball hadn't killed his son. This negligent son-of-a-bitch doctor, Gordon Brooks, had murdered him.

Quite naturally, this recreated truth took up residence in the enormous void in Doug's heart and soul. In no time at all, this newly minted reality put down roots and settled in like an old friend with every intention of remaining for a very long time.

Engrossed in these mental machinations, Doug never felt Vic's hand slide onto his shoulder. "Hey man, look." Vic offered a comforting squeeze. "That article doesn't mean a thing. You know how those reporters are. They're always sensationalizing everything--it just makes for a better story. I'm sure none of that has anything to do with Alex. Really, I'm sure of it."

Although completely still until that precise moment, Doug whipped his head around. He impaled the other man with his gaze. Vic recoiled, shocked by the depth of unveiled hatred he saw blazing in his friend's eyes. "Alex should never have died. Brooks killed him," Doug said with absolute conviction. "That bastard killed my son."

V

JOHN, ANXIOUS AND DISTRESSED, prowled around the cramped living room. He strode up and down, then back and forth as if trying to engrave some sort of bizarre pattern into the carpet. Eventually, overwhelmed by vertigo, he was forced to sit down.

Now needing to do something with his hands, he plucked a magazine from the coffee table. He rolled it up one way, then unfurled the slick pages and rerolled it in the opposite direction. A nervous tic pulled at the corner of his mouth. He couldn't remember the last time he had felt so distraught about anything. And to think, he was this agitated over nothing more complex than the simple act of telling the truth.

"This is exactly why people should never lie," he acknowledged aloud in the empty room. *How many times and to how many people had he expressed that simple truth to? Hundreds, definitely hundreds. And had he followed his own advice? Not even one little bit.* For weeks, no months, through Lord knew how many phone calls, he had intentionally deceived Natalie. In all this time, he had never told her he was a priest.

He pitched the periodical back onto the table. *How had he let this lie get so out of hand?* Although he had posed that question repeatedly, he had studiously avoided answering it. The best he could come up with was that the time never seemed right to tell her.

Garbage. That defense was complete crap and he knew it. The bottom line was he didn't want to tell her...he didn't want to confess the truth and risk having their relationship change.

Natalie back in his life had been unexpected and wonderful. He hadn't wanted it to end, which was... "Reprehensible," he told the living room furniture as he sprung from the chair and resumed his manic pacing once more.

He went round and round like a caged animal anticipating mealtime. He recalled the many conversations they'd had during the past two months; there had been dozens of opportunities for him to tell her the truth. They had discussed mundane and important topics alike.

Naturally, they had even talked at length about their individual careers. Although he had told her about much of the work he was involved in--projects with youth, the community, the local hospital--the words priest and church had remained mysteriously absent. He was a liar. A fraud. The guilt was killing him. But soon, all this was going to change. John was going to put an end to the lies, an end to the guilt. And very possibly, after his admission, Natalie would put an end to their new-found relationship.

Overcome once again by vertigo, John paused and leaned back against a wall. He slammed one balled fist onto the flat palm of his other hand. The priest checked his watch, then stared at the phone resting on the table. He willed it to ring, then swiftly adopted the opposing tack and willed it to never ring again.

John pushed off from the wall and went over to the window. He planted the heels of both hands on the sill, then bent closer to the glass as the final few vestiges of sunlight took refuge behind the distant horizon. Now, all that remained was a magnificent array of twilight hues. He savored the mixed palette of swirling shades.

A delicate strawberry pink interspersed with a peacock blue that melded as if by magic into a vibrant turquoise. And at the exact point where the sky met the land was the most brilliant blend of peach and lavender. The lovely colors brought peace to his heart and quieted his soul.

Behind him, the phone burst to life. Startled, John cracked his head against the window pane. He moved toward the table, massaging his scalp.

He gazed down at the shrilling phone as if it were a poisonous snake, coiling in preparation to strike.

Grabbing the receiver, he slid onto a chair. As expected, it was Natalie. Their conversation easily picked up where they had left off last time. They chatted for several minutes. Although John genuinely searched for an opportunity to segue into the topic of his real profession, somehow he just couldn't locate it. Or maybe, his inability to find the right point was less an issue of timing and more an issue of how Natalie sounded. Something about her voice wasn't quite right. In fact, the longer they talked, the worse it seemed.

In an effort to lighten the mood a little, John said, "So at the risk of being labeled a huge name-dropper, I have been working with a fairly famous person lately. Want to guess who it is?"

Natalie paused. "Okay, I'm game. Let's see, you live in Southern California. So I am going to go with the Chargers and...Drew Brees?"

John chortled at her response. "Pretty darn good guess but alas, wrong. It's Shea Lansing."

"No kidding. That is big-time name dropping. What are you doing with her?"

"Actually, I came to her as a consultant. She and her business people are laying the groundwork to start an organization to help homeless and orphaned children. She's trying to figure out what works, and importantly, what doesn't work in this area when it comes to kids."

"How great is that." Clearly intrigued, Natalie asked, "So, what is she really like?"

John thought about it. "Well, of course, she is spectacularly good-looking, you already know that. But I have got to tell you, the more you are around Shea, the less you notice her appearance. She is so much more than just a beautiful woman. She is smart, clever, interesting, and I guess the best thing of all, incredibly passionate. I have never seen anyone so focused on social change."

"Does she have a timeline for getting this thing started?"

"To the best of my knowledge, no. She's working toward some type of business degree, which should be completed soon. The start-up money is in place and it will be additionally funded by the proceeds from that sportswear line she recently launched."

"I've seen those clothes. They are sharp, very cutting edge. Definite budget-busters, though."

They chatted about Shea and the project a bit longer. Although Natalie had perked up somewhat initially, the previous lack-luster quality soon returned to her voice.

Finally, John proposed, "Listen, you sound totally done in this evening. Shall we call it a night? I can get back with you tomorrow?"

"No, I really need to talk to you now." To his astonishment, she began to weep, something he hadn't heard since their initial conversation. "Johnny, there's something I must tell you."

Alarmed, he sat up straight. "What is it?"

"Oh God. It's the reason I called you in the first place two months ago. But for as much as I've wanted to tell you, I just couldn't bring myself to do it. I didn't have the guts. But now I have no option."

A spasm of panic ran through him. His mind raced to conjure a variety of horrifying possibilities for what might be wrong. *Was she ill? A fatal disease?*

John repeated, "What is it, Natalie? Please tell me."

After a prolonged pause, Natalie blurted, "Johnny, you're a father."

Although his mind had offered up several options for what she might tell him, that definitely wasn't among them. He almost replied, "That's right, I am." That was what he had planned to tell her tonight. But now, she had said to him what he had wanted to say to her. *Did she somehow know he was a priest? How could it be? Wait … what? What was going on?*

Beyond confused, John held the phone away from him. He stared at it as if it were flotsam from outer space, some kind of foreign object never seen before. He must have misunderstood. "What did you say?"

Natalie's words came out in a rush, almost tripping over one-another. "Johnny, when you left Boston, I was pregnant. I was going to tell you after graduation. But then all that terrible stuff happened with your family. I decided to wait until a better time. But then you left."

She drew in a deep breath. "I almost had an abortion. I just couldn't go through with it. I guess there really is something to that Catholic guilt business. I decided to have the baby and give it up for adoption. But I couldn't do that either. I couldn't lose both of you." Her words cut off as abruptly as they had started and she recommenced crying.

In John's spartan living room, thousands of miles away from Natalie, indeed as far west as she was east, time stood suspended. He simply sat. Far more than stunned, he was literally paralyzed by Natalie's revelation. Never before had he experienced a shock of this magnitude. He was without resources upon which to draw.

Pregnant? Baby? The words would not, could not compute. It was just too much to take in.

"Johnny?"

He heard her speak, but could muster no response. The air around him had coagulated. She pressed him no further, merely joined him in silence.

Eventually, he asked, his voice little more than a whisper, "You were pregnant? You had a baby?" His throat felt dry as sand; his rasping voice sounded unfamiliar even to his own ears.

"Yes."

"But how?"

"Probably the usual way," she replied with a humorless snort.

"But we..."

"I know. When they say it only takes one time, they aren't kidding."

John was thrown completely off balance. He felt numb, removed, as though he wasn't really part of this situation at all. "I just can't believe it. I have no idea what to say."

"I know."

Several moments passed before he asked, "Why didn't you tell me?"

"How could I? I didn't know where you were. Even the letter you sent me had no return address."

An idea fluttered across his mind as John stared blankly at the ceiling. "My mother. Couldn't you have asked her?"

Natalie hesitated, then exhaled a deep sigh. "Johnny, your mother was really a mess for a long time after that thing with your dad. Remember how distant and peculiar she was right before you left? She only got worse. I went to the old house to talk to her. She wouldn't let me in. She just peeked at me through a crack in the door--it was really weird."

John still felt muddled as if his entire head was encased in cotton batting. Somehow, he managed to ask, "So she never knew, either?"

"No, never did. After I moved away, I rarely came back. Running into her two years ago was a complete fluke. And of course, I didn't have Elizabeth with me."

"Who?" John asked stupidly, having no idea who Natalie was talking about. "Elizabeth, my daughter," she clarified, before correcting herself, "Our daughter."

Dear Jesus. John slapped a hand over his eyes, her last two words reverberating in his brain? *Our daughter.* He couldn't believe it, he had a child, a girl. It was really too much. She must be..."How old is she?"

"Elizabeth will be sixteen on her next birthday."

"I have a fifteen-year-old daughter?"

"Yes, you do. And we must talk about her soon. Johnny, she needs you; we need you. But right now is probably not good. Why don't I give you a few days for this to sink in, then we can talk. Will that work for you?"

At this point, John would have agreed to anything. "Sure. Right. Good idea."

"Then I'll call you on Tuesday or Wednesday. Goodnight, Johnny."

He heard a click on her end of the line. The phone slipped from his fingers and fell to the floor with a soft thud. For a long time, John remained motionless in his chair, innervated by shock.

"I have a child," he told himself as the hazy room was swallowed up by total and complete darkness.

VI

NATALIE WEAVER CRADLED THE WHITE phone receiver, then ran her fingers across its smooth cool surface, imagining it was Johnny's face that she stroked. She heaved a weary sigh and rose from the edge of her queen-size bed. She moved aimlessly around the room, touching familiar possessions as if to reassure herself of their continued existence in her life.

In time, she made her way to a chair and lowered herself onto the peach flowered chintz fabric. She laid a forearm on the sill of the open bedroom window. Her face, which had settled into a mask of misery, broke into a smile at the fragrant aroma of freshly mown grass. Breathing deeply of the night air, she listened to the crickets energetically trumpeting their evening song. She peered into her large backyard, in the direction of their scarred and splintered redwood picnic table and the thicket of huge oaks that stood sentinel around her little herb garden. But she could see nothing through the pitch black.

Natalie contemplated what she'd just done. She had kept the secret for so long. Even now, she still wasn't sure if she had done the right thing. But maybe in situations such as this, no one was ever certain.

Understandably, Johnny had sounded so aghast. At least thank God, he hadn't sounded angry. Shock was one thing; contempt was something else altogether.

Faint amber light drifted in from the hall. Natalie could vaguely discern the brass picture frame resting atop a low chest of drawers. It showcased an ancient picture of her and Johnny, taken at a local carnival two weeks before their high school graduation. She was hugging a giant stuffed black-and-white panda that all but obscured her face and he was snuggled close, one arm wrapped around her shoulder. Both of their faces were defined by enormous smiles. Each was bursting with the excitement of the moment as well as the hope for the future that life offers only to the very young.

A shiver of sorrow and regret streaked through Natalie. If only their lives could have stopped right at that moment. If only they had been frozen in time and never had to experience the hell that was lying in wait just around the very next corner. But it didn't work that way--it never did.

She sucked in her lower lip. Tears slowly trickled down her cheeks, then splashed onto her hand. "Natalie, you are such an idiot," she reproached herself in the empty room. "You still love him." There, she had finally admitted it to herself. After all this time, she was still in love with her high school sweetheart.

And now he knew the truth about Elizabeth.

At the thought of her daughter, Natalie rose from the chair and walked barefoot into the hall. She paused at Elizabeth's door, listened and went into her room. Natalie picked her way through scattered clothing, shoes, magazines and other items of teenage detritus strewn on the floor, and edged over to the bed.

She gazed down at her slumbering child. In the dim light from the hall, Elizabeth appeared so young, so terribly innocent. Her tousled hair, so much like Natalie's own, fanned out behind her on the white pillowcase. The curled fingers of one hand were pressed against her pursed lips. Even in bed, she wore long sleeves to cover her arms.

How many wounds were hidden beneath that dark material? Natalie shuddered to imagine.

Unexpectedly, she was struck by a surge of such tremendous maternal love that she almost staggered on her feet. It occurred to her how very long it had been since she had felt anything so strong and poignant for her daughter.

Natalie realized how much she missed loving Elizabeth; the way she had when her daughter was young. Back when they'd shared special secrets and ice cream cones. When they'd discussed everything from how cows made milk to where the sun slept at night. When there was nothing Elizabeth wanted more in life than to spend time with her mom. Back then, loving Elizabeth had been the easiest, most wonderful thing in the whole world.

Now things were different. These days, fear was the dominant emotion in Natalie's heart, with love coming in at a distant second. Fear that Elizabeth might truly hurt herself. Fear that her daughter might die.

How had things ever gotten this bad?

She bent over the bed and kissed her daughter on the temple, then smoothed a stray strand of dark hair back away from her face. Natalie thought about how Elizabeth would react if she tried something like that during the day. There would be serious hell to pay. She rested her cheek against Elizabeth's hair, listening to her soft breathing. "You have no idea how much I love you," she whispered to her sleeping daughter.

Moments later, Natalie returned to her room to spend another restless night alone.

VII

JOHN MADE A FEW FINAL notations on the financial report, then spun around in a half circle to file the stapled papers. He caught sight of the young woman positioned in the doorway, just as she knocked on the jam with the knuckle of one crooked finger. "Mandy," he declared in astonishment. He tossed the report back onto his desk and jumped to his feet. "What a complete pleasure to see you here."

She gestured down the hall toward the front of the church. "The woman out there told me to just come back to your office. I hope it's okay."

"And I'm glad she did. Please, come in and sit."

John eyed her appreciatively while she walked in and took a seat across from his desk. Her long hair was swept into a French braid that cascaded down her back. She wore a knee-length red skirt with a matching shirt boasting a stylized white anchor on the front. Long white metal anchors also dangled from her ears. They swung to and fro with every step. "You certainly do look pretty this afternoon," He remarked as he reclaimed the chair behind his desk.

Mandy flung her purse onto the floor and settled back in the upholstered seat. She crossed her bare legs and propped both elbows on the chair arms "Thanks. I had to come into the city today and thought I would drop by. Do you have time to talk now? If you have something else, I could--"

"No, this is perfect. I needed a break from paperwork."

John scrutinized the young woman. He detected subtle signs of strain. Faint purple shadows underscored her lovely eyes and her face appeared pale and drawn. It occurred to him she even sounded somewhat flat and lack-luster, her voice having lost the effervescent lilt he previously associated with her. "What is it, something wrong?"

"Yes," she replied, staring down at her red leather sandal, her lightly mascaraed eyelashes casting spidery shadows onto her cheeks. "Something is very wrong, but I don't know what it is."

"With you?"

Mandy sighed, anxiety now figuring even more prominently in her expression. "No, I'm okay. It's Doug. There's something wrong with him."

John swiveled his chair from side to side. "Does it have to do with the loss of his son?"

Mandy bit the edge of her lower lip. "I'm pretty sure."

"But the last time I saw him, actually, both of you, he seemed to be doing well, as if he was really going to get on the other side of this tragedy."

"I know, that's what I thought, too." She lifted her eyes, which now glistened with unshed tears. "But then a couple of weeks later, something happened and he changed completely."

"In what way?"

"In every way. Honestly, he's like a man possessed, totally shut down. He never talks to anyone. He looks awful, like he is not eating or sleeping. It's as if some sort of darkness has closed in around him." She tilted her head to one side and a single tear escaped one eye. Mandy brushed it away with a swipe of the back of one hand.

"Are you sure this isn't just a normal manifestation of grief? I'm sure you know that people go through different stages."

"No. This isn't normal at all, something is definitely wrong."

John snagged his ball-point pen from the desk blotter. "But how do you know?" he persisted, absent-mindedly threading the pen through the fingers of his left hand.

Her hands dropped into her lap; she was the very picture of misery. "Because he really was getting better. After you left that day, we talked and even went through Alex's room together. Right after that, he returned to work. For a while, he was really doing well. You knew that Doug and I were sort of seeing each other, didn't you?"

"I assumed that."

She managed a faint, sad smile. "Well, I'm not saying we had anything big going, but there was certainly something there between us. We were dating, seeing each other regularly. Then all of the sudden, boom. It was done, over. Just like that."

Mandy rose and wandered over to a set of windows that opened out onto a tree-lined courtyard. She stood, her back to him, looking outside. The late afternoon sun limned the upper half of her body. After several moments, she turned around and leaned back against the sill. She pressed her palms together near her face in an attitude simulating prayer. "Please, don't get me wrong. This isn't one of those man-dumps-woman-and-woman-just-doesn't-get-it stories. Whether we had a future together or not, I would still be worried about him. And I'm not the only one. Everyone at work is concerned. No one knows what to do."

Pensive, the priest rubbed his chin. "What do they think it is?"

She lifted the dark braid, which had fallen forward over one shoulder and idly combed the loose tufts of hair at the end with her hooked fingers. "No one knows. Actually, I think Vic, one of his friends who works behind the front counter might have an inkling, but he won't talk about it."

"How can I help? What can I do?"

"Would you talk to him? Maybe you could find out what has happened." She pushed off from the sill, went back to her chair and retrieved the purse from the gray carpeted floor. "I know I have it here somewhere," Mandy muttered as she dug around inside the white straw bag. "Here it is." She drew out a slip of light-yellow paper from a side pocket and laid it on the edge of his desk. "Those are his phone numbers, both work and home."

She sat back down. "I'm sorry to ask you to do this, but honestly, I have nowhere else to turn."

"No, I'd be happy to call him. I'm going out of town in a few days, so I'll get to it right away," he assured her. "It just disturbs me to hear this type of news."

The room grew hushed. Mandy studied the man's face for a long time, then exhaled. In a sudden burst of candor, she declared, "Tell you what, you don't look all that good yourself. In fact, you look kind of crummy."

The moment the words left her lips, she gave a little gasp. Her cheeks blushed scarlet. "Please forgive me for saying that. I'm sure it's none of my business."

"And why not?" Humor twinkled in his dark brown eyes.

"Well, because, because," she sputtered, then burst into laughter. She regained some of her natural insouciance, finally sounding like the Mandy he knew. "Because I don't know why not. Somehow, it seems as if you're just never supposed to say anything personal to a priest. Like they're different from everybody else. Like they don't wear underpants, or something."

"Uh-huh."

She flashed a bright smile. "Wow, isn't that just a bunch of crap?"

"Should you be saying crap?" John tossed her a mischievous wink.

The two laughed together before Mandy repeated, "You really don't look very happy."

He shifted in his seat. "Didn't know it showed."

"Well, it does." She gave a curt nod of her head, which sent the miniature anchor earrings into a frenzy of activity. "So, what's up? Want to tell me about it? I'm a good listener."

"I bet you are, and I do appreciate the offer. Actually, I think I can work it out on my own, but thanks anyway."

Mandy rose. "You bet. But if you ever change your mind, I included my number on that paper. You can call me anytime. I never thought about it before, but I imagine priests must get awfully lonely sometimes."

John felt tears sting his eyes. "We do. We really do."

VIII

DOUG SIDLED UP TO THE vacant park bench and lowered himself onto the slatted wood seat. He slung his right foot on top of the opposing left knee. Behind mirrored sunglasses, his eyes swept back and forth along the lengthy stretch of sidewalk on the opposite side of the street.

He congratulated himself on the selection of this location. This particular bench was perfect, affording him a clear, unimpeded view of the entire street. Doug swiveled his wrist and checked the time. Wouldn't be long, now. Idly, he ran a thumb across his bare upper lip where a moustache had always resided; but now, the thumb only encountered bare flesh.

Although the day was bathed in toasty sunlight, Doug was as frozen as a glacier. His thoughts were cold, his body frigid. If he had possessed a heart, it would be a solid block of ice. But his heart was gone now, leaving only a dim memory of its existence. So the chill simply extended its frosty fingers to embrace the empty cavity inside his chest where a heart had once resided.

As time marched along, several people Doug knew passed by. But few noticed him sitting on the park bench, so anonymous was he in his newly acquired shades, faded jeans, and nondescript T-shirt. This treasured anonymity only validated what he felt inside. With every passing day, Doug felt less and less like himself, the Doug he once was. Now he was another person, a man defined by hate. It burned like an omnipresent black ember deep inside of him. This new-found hate had ultimately proven his salvation for it had obliterated the wrenching sense of loss.

The transformation had taken time. The initial rage at the doctor's guilt had lacked direction. It expanded within his soul like bubbling water in an overheated radiator. It threatened to explode any moment and blow him to bits.

Finally, the fury consolidated and streaked in one direction: revenge. He would kill the man, and therefore rectify the unspeakable wrong. With that, the despair vanished. Simultaneously, hate rushed in to fill the vacuum. It also took on a life of its own. Now it was both a part of him, yet separate from him. Inside him, yet standing alongside him like a ubiquitous shadow.

Doug knew there wouldn't be a "him" again until the doctor was dead.

He folded his arms over his chest and shifted his weight a bit on the bench. He thought about how easily everything had coalesced. The plan had simply come to him as if providential. Perhaps the Almighty had appointed him to exact holy retribution on earth.

It certainly seemed more than coincidental that Brooks would soon be leaving town. It took little effort to extract the details from the doctor's support staff.

Exactly how to commit the murder had niggled at Doug for a while. Then, sprawled on his disheveled bed one night, caught in that fuzzy, dreamlike state between awake and asleep, he just knew. The plan was clear, refined to the most intricate detail. Now he just had to knock out a couple of details.

From the corner of one eye, Doug caught a glimpse of the approaching man. He sprang cat-quick from the bench and hopped into the street. Jaywalking to the opposite side, he picked up his quarry mid-block. As the man passed, Doug fell into line directly behind him. They stopped at a light, then crossed the street. He made his move as they stepped from the gutter to the curb. "Nice dog," he commented with feigned enthusiasm.

The blind man thanked him, then walked on down the sidewalk. The guide dog at his side deftly maneuvered the foot traffic.

Doug matched the man stride for stride and kept the conversation alive. "What's his name?"

"Shelby," the man supplied, then added, "He's a Golden Retriever."

Damned dumb-ass name, Doug thought to himself, eyeing the dog who was a deep russet in color with wide shoulders and a long body.

"Ridiculous name, isn't it?" It was as though the dog's owner had actually overheard Doug's private musings.

At that, Doug spontaneously laughed. It was a sound he hadn't heard in quite some time. "Honest to God, I was just thinking the exact same thing,"

The man shrugged in blatant resignation. "The dogs come named," he added, by way of explanation. "Not much you can do since they've had that moniker all their lives."

The trio came to a stop again at the next light and Doug inquired, "Where did you get Shelby?"

The man extended a hand and stroked the dog's head. Responding, Shelby gazed up at his master with huge, adoring eyes. "From the guide dog school; it's right outside San Francisco."

"You know, I was wondering something about these dogs. Maybe you'd know the answer."

"Sure, what is it?"

"My mom lives in northern California and has a friend with a dog just like yours. It could use a new one of these things." He reached down and tapped the handle, which was clutched tightly in the blind man's left hand.

"A harness?"

"Yeah, that's it. Evidently, the current one is all banged up and my mom would like to buy a new one for her as a gift. But she doesn't know how or where to get it."

"What a nice thing for your mother to do. Sure, I can help. In fact, look right here." With his right hand, the man pointed to the brown leather strap arcing over the dog's back. "The phone number for the school is embossed right there. Your mother could call and order it."

The light changed to green. Vehicles and a handful of pedestrians surged forward, while the two men and dog remained on the curb. Doug squatted down and peered closer at the harness strap.

Shelby, viewing the action as an invitation, swung his golden head over. He nuzzled Doug's neck, his bushy tail sweeping the air behind him. "You're as bad as Sam," he told the dog before locating the number and committing it to memory. Doug couldn't resist—he gave Shelby a quick scratch behind the ear.

Doug stood back up. "Hey, thanks for the help." He hesitated, then, as if the question had just that very moment entered his mind, asked, "Can you also order those plaid raincoat type things from the same place? I've seen your dog wearing one on occasion."

"You bet. Some people think they're a pain in the rear end, but for as much rain as we get on the island, I'd hate to be without it."

"Great. My mom will be real pleased. Thanks again, for the information."

"No problem, happy to help. If you have any more questions, stop me anytime."

Doug said good-bye to the twosome and headed home.

Later, Doug wandered from his small kitchen into the family room. He flopped onto the couch. Fatigue overwhelmed him. He closed his eyes and briefly rubbed his forehead, then flung the arm over the edge of the couch.

Sam, spying the available hand, ambled over and poked his snout into the palm. He nudged the hand, trying to flip it onto the crown of his head. A good scratch would be welcome. Sam paused mid-nudge. He gave the palm a serious once-over with his highly discriminating nose, then glared at Doug, clearly indignant at discovering another dog's scent. The look went unobserved. Sam wandered away and emitted a disgruntled sigh as he plopped down behind a nearby chair.

The sigh also went unnoticed. Doug merely lifted the offending hand, slid it between his head and the couch cushion and massaged the back of his neck. He rolled his head this way and that in an effort to relieve accumulated tension. A small smile flitted across his face as he reviewed the events of the past hour. Acquiring the necessary information had proven infinitely easier than expected. The order had been placed; he should have the paraphernalia for Sam in no time at all.

The gun and airline tickets were purchased. The dark hair dye was waiting in the medicine cabinet. Once Sam's new wardrobe arrived, he would have just enough time to acquaint the dog with his new role before the flight.

Samson masquerading as a seeing-eye dog was hard to imagine, but Doug had surreptitiously observed the blind man long enough now. He felt he and Sam could pull it off.

Propping a heel on the table in front of him, the man endeavored to clear his mind of all thought. Soon, the tension ebbed. He envisioned himself floating on a pontoon on the surface of a tranquil sea. He imagined hot sun pouring down onto his skin, filling him with much-needed warmth. Floating... just floating...

The sound of the kitchen phone stabbed through the room like the crack of a bullwhip. The brief flirtation with sleep had left Doug momentarily paralyzed. Thoughts muzzy, he stared blankly at the ceiling. The bell rang a second time and Doug's weary mind made the connection. It was the phone.

He got to his feet and stumbled over to the kitchen, ripping the receiver from its wall mount halfway through the third ring. "Yeah," Doug said to the unknown caller.

Miles away, sitting at his desk, John had placed the call. When the phone was answered, the priest lurched forward in his chair and snatched the slip of paper from the desktop where he had tossed it moments earlier. Surely, he had dialed the number correctly. But he must have made an error. "I'm sorry, but I believe I've misdialed," He confessed to the stranger at the other end, an apologetic note evident in his voice.

"What number did you want?"

John read the number printed on the note and the man replied, "You've got it."

"Doug?"

"Yeah, who is this?"

John fell silent, stunned by the realization that this man was actually Doug Sanders. His voice sounded more than hollow, far more than merely remote, it sounded...dead. Aghast by the thought, the priest fairly stuttered, "Its John, John Larken."

Now the silence lived on the other end of the phone. "Father John," he added as an afterthought.

Alone in his kitchen, Doug repeated, "John." Still dazed, he slid onto a barstool. His elbow knocked an empty beer can over onto its side. It fell off the edge of the counter and plummeted to the floor, bounced twice, then rolled beneath a cabinet. Doug drummed his fingers on the countertop, trying to unscramble his muddled thoughts. *John, did he know someone named John? His father? But both his parents had been dead for years.* Finally, one key thought separated from all the rest and sprang to the forefront of his mind: priest. That was it. He was the priest from the hospital. "Oh yeah, Jesus, sure," Doug acknowledged. "What do you want?"

"I was just calling to see how you are," came the reply.

Doug felt light-headed. Shit, he was so exhausted. "Fine, I'm doing fine."

"Are you sure you're okay?" the priest persisted.

"Yes, I'm doing okay...now."

"Now? But I thought you seemed to be doing well last time I saw you, remember several weeks ago when we had hot chocolate and talked about the experience you had on the beach? Has something else happened since then?"

Doug tried to recall when he had last seen the priest. Christ, it seemed like years, not weeks. "Sure, I remember seeing you, and I remember talking about that seagull. But turns out, I was wrong about that situation."

"Why do you think that?"

"Remember how I thought God was trying to tell me something? Well he was," Doug paused in his explanation and released a humorless chuckle. It was a ghastly sound that made John shudder on the opposite end of the phone line. "But I had it all wrong. I didn't figure out what he really wanted me to know until later."

"And what was that? What did God want you to know?"

Doug thought about his response. Although his initial inclination was to dissemble, he suddenly reconsidered. Why not speak the truth? After all, he was a priest. What was he going to do...tell? He couldn't. It had something to do with their vows or some other bullshit like that.

"Just between you and me?"

"Sure," John replied.

Doug divulged, "He wanted me to know that Gordon Brooks, that son-of-a-bitch doctor, murdered my son. And now I'm going to kill his ass."

IX

SHEA SAT CROSS-LEGGED ON the cushioned table dressed in a white gown. She inspected her surroundings. To say the room was a far cry from the sterile, austere exam rooms she'd known as a child would be one of the greater understatements of the decade.

It was the absolute antithesis of anything she'd ever seen before. The textured walls were spangled with framed prints depicting serene English landscapes, lush plants draped from every possible shelf and the floor was blanketed with a plush forest-green carpet. This deep hue was replicated in the patterned fabric on the room's one upholstered chair as well as on the sheet covering the table upon which Shea sat. Even the light oak magazine rack on the wall to her left was trimmed in a rich green lacquer.

Shea perused the selection in the rack and plucked out a favorite fashion magazine. She idly leafed through its glossy pages. Toward the middle, she stumbled upon the full-page ad for Image shampoo. It was the first time she'd seen the ad, and by God if that darn fountain, which had been dull as paste to look at, didn't just work beautifully as a backdrop.

Who would have figured it? And the lighting had been just right. The late-afternoon sun had reflected off the spray, causing it to shimmer like a thousand shards of glass, creating a halo effect.

Of course, Connor had been right about which photo they would ultimately select for the kick-off ad in the national campaign. The client had chosen one of his. And no wonder. Although Todd's photos were technically perfect, Connor's shots had captured love. It was impossible to miss. This raw emotion radiated from Shea's smile and glittered in her eyes. Naturally, a casual viewer would subliminally correlate this almost palpable adoration with a bottle of shampoo.

Shea knew better. All that love had been reserved exclusively for the photographer—him and him alone.

She closed the magazine and thought about Connor. Although she hadn't realized it at the time of the Image shoot, she certainly knew it now: she was head-over heels in love with him. The concept almost made her blush. She had never been in love before. She was constantly overwhelmed, not only by the magnitude, but the depth of the feeling.

With all its wonder, it had also proven difficult for her. The advent of love in her life had forced her to reconsider and ultimately reframe many of her previously held beliefs, especially regarding men. It required her to resurrect a galaxy of painful emotions long dead in her heart. But she was making huge progress. Connor's patience seemed to know no bounds.

Suddenly, the door swung open, causing a startled Shea to pop up on the table. "Looks as if I caught you daydreaming," the large woman remarked as she lumbered across the room, her stethoscope swinging from side to side like an elephant's trunk.

"You certainly did; I was a million miles away."

The doctor came to a stop next to the table and extended one meaty arm. "I'm Lucille Drexler."

Shea shook the outstretched hand. "It's nice to meet you, Dr. Drexler."

"Call me Lucille, everyone does."

Shea felt at ease with this woman. Maybe it was because she looked so much like the grandmother she'd always wanted. "Okay, I will. I got your name from a friend of mine, Candis John."

The doctor's forehead creased in concentration. "I haven't seen Candis for a while, except in there." She waved a plump hand toward the magazines. "In fact, half my patients are in those pages on any given month. Sometimes I hardly recognize them, given all the makeup they pile on."

The doctor whirled around with a tremendous amount of grace for a woman her size and bustled over to the chair. She seated herself and slapped the patient chart onto her ample lap. "Now let me just see," she murmured as she scanned the information on the chart through tortoise-shell glasses. She ran an index finger down the top sheet as she spoke. "I see you're not feeling quite up to snuff. Why don't you tell me about it?"

Shea delineated the problem, repeating nearly word for word what she'd told the nurse minutes earlier. She detailed the extreme fatigue, the malaise, the flu-like symptoms and the aching joints. "I just don't know what it could be. I'm usually so healthy--full of energy," Shea eventually concluded, "I've just never felt so bad for so long."

The doctor ran a hand through her short-cropped gray hair. She asked Shea about her family background, congenital diseases, sleep, exercise and eating habits, other medications and more as she worked her way through the pages of the chart. "I see here that you don't take the pill."

"No, never have."

"Do you use contraceptives?"

"No, not right now," Shea replied and felt a slight flush beginning to creep up her neck. "Well, actually, not ever. But I've met someone very special so I may come back to you sometime soon to get a prescription."

Lucille swung her head in Shea's direction and gave her a penetrating look. "So you're not currently involved sexually, but are considering it?"

Shea fiddled with the hem of the white gown. "Yes, that's right. I've never been involved with anyone in that way before." She offered the doctor a diffident smile. "If there's only one virgin left in the universe, it's me."

The doctor gave a curt, approving nod. "Nothing wrong with that. In today's disease-ridden climate, I wish I had about a thousand more of you. Then I wouldn't have to worry quite as much." To Shea's relief, Lucille moved on, now inquiring about previous hospitalization or surgeries.

"I've only had one surgery. It was a few years ago. I was eighteen; I was doing a layout for these new safari type clothes. We went to Africa for the shoot," Shea explained and screwed up her face in distaste as she recalled the hellish experience. "It had rained in the jungle for the longest time. On the last day, the jeep I was in hit a slick patch of road and overturned. My spleen ruptured; they had to remove it."

Lucille tapped her ballpoint pen against one fleshy cheek. "Doesn't surprise me at all. Spleens never take too kindly to extreme trauma. Did they do the surgery there?"

"Unfortunately, they had to. I was bleeding internally. It couldn't wait."

"Extreme blood loss?" The doctor raised one gray-flecked eyebrow in question.

Shea nodded. "Buckets. Lots of transfusions. And though Africa isn't exactly the place I'd choose to have surgery again, I guess they did an okay job. I had to have the scar revised later because I do so many swimsuit layouts, but now it hardly shows. Occasionally it is air brushed out of a photo. No big deal."

As Shea watched from her perch on the table, Lucille bent over her clipboard, jotted a notation on the chart, then circled it with a flourish. "You know, I believe I vaguely recall those advertisements. Seems to me they had wild animals in them, didn't they?"

"Yep, those were the ones." Shea propped one shoulder against the wall and rolled her eyes. "And I had always thought working with egotistical male models was challenging. Tell you what, men are a piece of cake next to those big cats. And I was supposed to look happy and carefree like it was just an everyday walk in the park."

Lucille got to her feet and tossed the chart aside. "I know you girls work hard."

After completing a cursory exam, the doctor said, "Your glands, heart, lungs, basically everything looks about right. I'm going to run a battery of blood tests to see what's going on. "

"When will you have the results?"

"Should be just a few days. We'll schedule an appointment to go over what we found."

"Actually, I have a job in New York coming up. I will be gone for several days."

"No problem." Lucille retrieved the chart from the chair and headed for the door. "Just make it for when you get back.

"Okay, I will." The patient hopped down from the table.

"Have a good trip. See you in a week or so." The doctor stepped into the hall.

"Thanks," Shea called after her, then got back into her clothes, her mind already leaping to her next appointment.

X

AS DAY GRADUALLY EBBED INTO night, the old building underwent the standard evening rituals. Lights were switched off. Occupants exited. Doors were shut tight and locked. Now the church was utterly silent, save for an occasional shudder or creak emanating from rickety boards as the ancient building settled in for the long night ahead.

In his shadowy office, John sat as still as the structure surrounding him. Only an occasional troubled exhalation issued from between his lips as he replayed the recent conversation over and over again in his mind. He still could not quite take in what he had just heard. Doug Sanders, a man he'd spent time with, shared grief and even discussed God with, was planning to kill Dr. Brooks?

Grim-faced, John shook his head. It was as shocking as anything he had ever heard; and he'd heard a lot during the past few years. What's more, John had absolutely no doubt as to Doug's sincerity. The only thing he didn't know was when he planned on carrying out this heinous act. Doug had indicated it wouldn't be for quite some time. Now the priest wondered if that had been a ruse simply to hold any immediate action at bay. John desperately hoped no plans were in place. He needed time to figure out what to do.

He gnawed on the tip of one thumb. Should he call the police? The moment the question presented itself, he jettisoned it, knowing it was not a viable option. The only other person he could ethically discuss this problem with was Pat and he was out of town on church business.

After considering the situation from every possible vantage point, he concluded only one option existed--he would have to wait until he could speak to Pat. Still, he couldn't get that horrific conversation out of his mind, the flat quality of Doug's voice, the venomous nature of his words, the extraordinary intensity of his hatred.

John shivered, a chill darting up his spine. It was the most taxing interaction he'd ever taken part in, with the single exception of the phone call last week with Natalie. Nothing would or could ever eclipse the shock he had felt at discovering he was a father.

The priest slammed his palms onto the armrests of his chair, propelled himself to his feet and strode the length of the office. His mind leaped back to his daughter, a topic he had been consumed with for days. He recalled Natalie's description of Elizabeth as a young child. A portrait had been painted of an energetic, precocious little girl with a sunny disposition, inquisitive mind and robust little body. In recent conversations, Natalie had regaled him with at least half-a-dozen delightful stories about Elizabeth when she was young. John had loved hearing these poignant tales; and now, he held them close to his heart, treasuring them as Natalie had for years.

Yet, as he paced up and down the quiet office, hands jammed into pants pockets, he forced his mind to move forward, closer to the present. In a recent conversation, Natalie had described the gradual transformation from adorable child into recalcitrant teenager. The mood-swings. The defiance. The self-absorption.

Natalie had hated the onset of this new Elizabeth. However, she acknowledged these changes were a normal and quite natural part of a girl growing up. But only to a certain extent.

By her fifteenth year, Elizabeth had reached, then far surpassed, that point. Her grades plummeted. Her attitude reached a new low. She no longer cared about her own appearance. Worst of all, her circle of friends altered radically. Natalie, accustomed to the fresh-faced, cheerful girls of

Elizabeth's younger years, was shocked to discover this new breed of female her daughter was now hanging out with. They were sullen, morose creatures whose attitude was as black as their clothing.

Natalie did everything possible to help her daughter. But nothing worked. Elizabeth continued on a downward spiral.

"I was at my wit's end," Natalie had confided to John. "My daughter was falling apart right in front of me and I could do nothing to help her. Then one day I came across your phone number. I realized that you might be the only one who could save Elizabeth from herself. That's when I first called you."

"Then why didn't you tell me about her sooner?"

It was the strangest thing; shortly after I first contacted you, Elizabeth rallied. For a brief time, she was her old self again. I thought perhaps all the things I'd already done, the counseling, the long talks, had finally sunk in. I was wrong.

"After five or six weeks, she slipped back into this self-destructive behavior once again. It's even worse now. I've found pills in her backpack and she has started to cut."

Bewildered, John had asked, "Cut classes?"

"Cut herself. With razor blades. Johnny. It's bad. We have to do something about this soon, together...the two of us."

"The two of us," John whispered aloud as his frantic pacing ceased. He leaned back against his desk, arms folded over one another, hands gripping his elbows. Now standing still, he was acutely aware of the wild fluttering of his heart in his chest. John thought of how often that had been happening lately. Without warning and seemingly without reason, his heart would simply spring forth with a burst of energy. This manic stuttering would continue for several seconds, then cease.

Too much stress and worry, he decided. He returned to the previous thought, repeating a second time, "The two of us." A sad smile crept onto his face. He liked the sound of that simple phrase far too much.

In their final conversation, he and Natalie decided he would come back for a visit. They would meet in New York and spend some time together, without their daughter. They would settle on a course of action. He still hadn't told her about being a priest.

Decisions, John thought soberly to himself, *so many decisions.* The most critical of all being that of the priesthood, whether to remain or go. He wanted to determine the answer to that question prior to the trip back East. But time was running out.

John's shoulders drooped. He hung his head and sighed in exhaustion. He dropped his face into his open palms. "Oh dear Lord, what am I going to do?" he asked in a voice riddled with despair as the last ember of twilight died and the empty room tumbled into total darkness.

PART V

August, 2002, Seconds

After Flight 1012 Struck

Mount Miguel

I

THE SEVERED SECTION OF THE American Air jet spiraled several hundred feet down the side of the mountain; an enormous plume of white sparks fanned out behind it like a brilliant rooster tail. In its wake, it left hunks of twisted metal, airplane seats, scattered pieces of luggage, and a host of mangled body parts. The intense friction caused several random brushfires to ignite behind the fractured fuselage.

The jet tail skidded to a stop and perched precariously on an outcropping of jagged rocks where the land leveled off. After the ear-splitting screech of metal scraping along the rocky terrain, the subsequent quiet was riveting in its intensity, save for the occasional whine of steel as the broken aircraft settled more comfortably into its new home.

Disconcerted by the eerie silence, Sabrina Walsh opened her eyes. She stared for long moments at the strange object positioned three or four inches from her face. Flummoxed, the flight attendant scowled, trying to establish what it was. Sabrina knew she'd seen this thing before. In fact, she'd seen it quite recently. In a flash of recognition, it came to her. It was a shoe, one of the white leather shoes her friend, Shelly, always wore when she worked.

Inundated with a profound sense of accomplishment for identifying the mysterious object, the attendant allowed her eyes to slide shut once more. Dealing with that shoe situation had thoroughly exhausted her. She needed to give her eyes a little rest, just a minute or two. A moment later, a splintered pane of glass fell from a nearby window. It struck Sabrina on the back, jolting her from the dream-like state.

Her eyes snapped open. Now she saw not only the shoe, but the foot sprouting from its leather edge. Quite naturally, she followed the line of progression from foot to ankle, ankle to leg, leg to knee. Her gaze stopped there, having nowhere else to go. There was no more leg.

Confused panic streaked through Sabrina. She struggled to sit upright, only to discover the upper half of her body was pinned between two airplane seats. Ragged breaths expelled from her mouth as she extricated herself from the bondage. Finally, she managed to ease into a semi-sitting position.

The young woman gaped at the carnage surrounding her. Her body began to shiver in shock, her teeth chattered.

Sheer chaos was everywhere. Seats were torn from their moorings and overturned, windows were blown out, and passengers were strewn in haphazard positions like rag dolls dumped from a toy box. Fragments of splintered glass, winking in the morning sunlight, blanketed every surface. Debris in the form of clothing, books, and handbags was scattered everywhere. Gritty dust was ushered through the cabin by random gusts of wind.

An item dangling from one of the overhead bins caught Sabrina's roving gaze. She squinted, transfixed by the object swinging languidly in the breeze. The dust made it difficult to identify. She squinted harder and eventually made it out. It was a woman's lacy undergarment, a light-peach underwire bra.

Oh my God, it's a push-up bra. A lunatic expression spread across Sabrina's cut and bruised face. Maniacal giggles bubbled up in her throat. Her self-control was rapidly slipping away. Right now all she wanted to do was sit back and have a good hard belly laugh. Just laugh and laugh and laugh.

At that moment, she caught sight of the giant ball of fire and black smoke billowing in the distant sky. As if someone had just cracked her across the face with an open palm, the hysteria was replaced by the realization of what that black cloud meant. The jet fuel had exploded. Everyone in the front of the plane must be dead.

Sabrina gasped out loud. "Meredith. Oh no, Meredith," she croaked, staring dumbfounded at that horrible dark smoke.

The aircraft beneath her lurched violently, emitting a shrill screech as it tilted to an even more unstable angle on the rocks. Sabrina's attention was yanked back to the present. *What was she doing? Had she forgotten all her training? She had to help the others in this section of the plane.*

Suddenly, she was seized by an atavistic horror. What if there were no others? What if she were the only survivor? "Oh God, please let there be more, please not just me," the attendant prayed aloud in the stillness.

Moving with haste, she insinuated a hand between her thighs and belly, endeavoring to reach the release on her seatbelt. It had remained intact throughout the ordeal and probably saved her life. She fumbled for several seconds, driven on by the urgent need to see to the passengers. Finally, it clicked open.

Sabrina eased to the edge of her seat cushion. Only then did she connect with the agonizing pain radiating from nearly all points of her body. Her left arm, probably broken, could do nothing but hang limply at her side. The piercing pain in her chest suggested one if not several ribs were cracked. There were at least half-a-dozen areas from which she was actively bleeding. But as she clambered to her feet, she discovered her legs had not been hurt.

Standing straight, intense dizziness overtook her, threatening to pull her back down. She swooned and gritted her teeth against the pain. The attendant pressed a hand to one cheek, fingertips grazing a deep gash at her temple. Although the hand came away drenched in blood, the sight impacted her not in the least.

Disassociated, she stared down at the sticky dark substance, then absent-mindedly wiped it off on the bodice of her already blood-spattered uniform. Far more concerned about the other survivors as well as the continued integrity of the damaged aircraft, Sabrina crept forward. With deliberate care, she picked her way through the litter.

A restroom door had ripped free from its hinges and was flattened on top of someone. Sabrina hobbled over to it. *Another dead body,* she thought, but wanted desperately to be wrong. *Maybe it was the rest of Shelley?* Sabrina lifted the broken door a foot or so.

From out of nowhere, a flash vision of the Avon lady waiting on the other side of the door zipped through the woman's brittle mind. Hysteria threatened a second time. She imagined the doorbell's familiar bing-bong chime. Sabrina opened her mouth with every intention of saying "Avon calling" at the appropriate moment. Only with the greatest exertion of will did she hold back. A crazy grin tugging at the corners of her mouth, Sabrina allowed herself only one minor giggle before yanking the door into the air.

The door felt heavy in her hand. No, no perky Avon lady or Shelley on the floor, there was just another mangled corpse ensconced in more debris.

Vertigo swept over Sabrina. She dropped the door. A miserable groan of physical and emotional pain peeled from her lips. Clenching and unclenching one fist at her side, she gazed about, trying to gauge the optimal route out of this confined space and into what remained of the cabin. Scrabbling for purchase, she stepped over the door. The attendant gingerly waded through a mountain of clothes, cups and trays. Her good arm flailed through the air, seeking any possible hand-hold.

Moments later, she stumbled into the passenger area, her eyes strafing the wreckage for survivors. The sound of the whistling wind raked across her overwrought nerves. "Hello," she called stupidly, her voice thready and weak. No one answered, but the attendant thought she caught a glimpse of movement closer to the front. She staggered toward it.

Halfway there, she stopped and peered down into a passenger's face. The woman's head was propped up against an adjoining seat. She looked as if she were gazing out at the ghastly tar-black cloud, just as Sabrina had done minutes earlier. "Are you all right? Can I help you?" the attendant asked, a note of excitement underscoring her words. Yet, those sightless eyes were destined to stare at that distant sky for all of eternity. A plank of steel had embedded itself in the woman's chest, nearly splitting her body in two. Sabrina quickly averted her gaze, but it wasn't fast enough. She knew that horrifying image would be engraved on her mind for the rest of her life.

Tottering on the ripped carpet, she forged ahead, finally reaching the area where she thought a passenger might be alive. Her anxious eyes darted around, looking for someone, anyone she could help. "Hello, is anyone..." Her plea faded away as each word was whisked off by the playful breeze.

Overwhelmed by a sense of complete desolation, she stood motionless at the edge of the shredded aircraft. Her head and shoulders drooped, both arms dangled ineffectually at her sides. Her unsteady breathing punctured the silence. Far in the distance came the strains of approaching sirens. *And they'll only find me, no one else. I'm the only one left,* she thought in despair, staring at the scrubby landscape below.

"I'm down here. Please help me," a muffled voice called out from somewhere behind her.

Sabrina spun around. Her feet got caught up in the rubble. "Where, where are you?" she asked, euphoria flooding through her at the sound of another human voice, the thought of another survivor.

"Here."

The attendant stooped down and saw a man wedged beneath an upside-down seat. "Hold on, I'll help you." She threaded one arm around the seat and pulled. The man groaned in terrible pain. "Shit, shit, oh shit," she muttered as she approached the recalcitrant seat from a different angle. This time, when she yanked from the opposite direction, the seat arced back, then rolled off him.

She fell to her knees beside the passenger, who was lying on his back, face contorted by pain. "I'm so sorry. I didn't mean to hurt you." Sabrina knelt over him and began to weep. Huge tears splashed onto his ashen cheeks and neck, cutting deep furrows into the grimy skin.

Gordon raised a hand and patted her forearm. "I know you didn't. And I'm all right, much better now with that thing off me."

She clutched his hand, her sticky blood smearing over his palm. "Good, I'm glad."

"What happened?" he asked. "I was asleep and..."

Sabrina's face clouded in concentration as she struggled to recall. "I don't know, I can't really remember, either," she finally managed in a voice riddled with confusion. "We had an engine fire—I remember that. The plane crashed, but I don't know..."

"How are the rest?" Gordon struggled to sit up. White-hot pain tore through his lower body. "Maybe I could help. I'm a doctor."

Sabrina shuddered. Her breath came in ragged hitches and her subsequent reply issued forth in sharp staccato bursts. "I don't know. A lot are dead. You're the only one I've found. There might be others. I need to check again. Can you move?"

Gordon propped himself up onto his elbows and stared down at his lower limbs, staggered by what he saw. The sharp edges of panic reached out for him. He struggled to keep hysteria at bay. "I think both my legs are broken. I probably won't be much help."

She tracked his line of vision and sucked in a sharp breath. "Oh Jesus God, your legs," Sabrina wailed as a tic began convulsing at the corner of one eye. Her teeth resumed their wild clacking, now sounding absurdly loud in the quiet cabin.

He clamped a steadying grip on her forearm. "Look, you need to go and check on the others," he pronounced the words with exaggerated care. "See if anyone needs help. I could make my way back if I have to."

Blinking several times, Sabrina nodded. "Yes, that's what I'll do. You stay right here. Don't go anywhere. I'll go see." She used her good hand for leverage, then scrambled to her feet. The attendant teetered crazily as another wave of dizziness hit her like a sledgehammer.

"You okay?"

"Yeah, sure, fine. I'm going now." She stepped over Gordon and gaining a foothold, launched herself back down the aisle.

There was at least one other survivor besides herself. This knowledge made her less frantic in her search. She moved from row to row. After a while, she became inured to the sight of disfigured and dead bodies. Death was everywhere. Yet, her composure disintegrated completely when she stumbled upon the little boy, who was still strapped in the window seat. His head was twisted into an impossible, almost obscene, angle. Even Sabrina, with her untrained eye, knew his neck was broken.

"Oh no," Sabrina whimpered in a quavering voice as she gazed into the sweet countenance, which still wore the thick coke-bottle eyeglasses. A vivid mental image of this boy, smiling and laughing as he colored a purple dinosaur picture with the passenger in the next seat just prior to take off, remained in her mind.

Now, she looked at the man sitting alongside the dead child. He was slumped over in his seat, blood dripping onto his burgundy shirt from a deep laceration near one ear. She shook his shoulders and spoke close to his bent head. No response. Probably dead, too, Sabrina decided, giving up and moving on.

From his position on the floor, Gordon heard the attendant cry out and could only imagine the horrors she must be encountering. His inaction was unacceptable. He struggled to a sitting position once more. Fiery pain ripped through his shattered legs, causing him to gray out. Sweat dripped down his face. Gordon leaned all his weight on the heels of both hands and looked about, hoping to find someone he might help.

A man's crumpled body was near him on the floor. Only half of his face was visible beneath one outstretched arm. Gordon had a dim memory of this man early in the flight. There was something unusual, special about him. That was it. He was the blind man with the dog. Gordon surveyed the carnage. No sign of the black dog. Undoubtedly it was sucked right out of the jagged opening, which was mere inches from their seats.

The blind man's dark glasses had been knocked off. They were lying close to the curled fingers of his open hand, one mirrored lens now missing. Reflexively, Gordon's hand flew to his face, reassuring himself of the continued presence of his own eyeglasses.

Gordon edged toward the other passenger, teeth clenched against the breathtaking pain. Halfway to his destination, he paused and submitted to the agony. Hot tears spilled from his eyes and mingled with the sweat streaming down his face.

Eyes closed, he grew aware of the drone of an industrious bee as it buzzed through the cabin. Gordon was incredulous. *How could a bee, a common, garden-variety bee possibly be part of this hellish scene? It would be like a clown at a gravesite, an undertaker at a wedding. Certain things were just unacceptable...beyond the pale.* He allowed the thought to inundate him for only a moment before resuming his journey.

The doctor, smothering a gasp of exquisite pain, swallowed hard; he closed the gap between himself and the other man.

At first, Gordon felt certain the man was dead; by all rights, he certainly should be. The chest and abdominal wounds were as severe as any he'd ever seen. The blood loss was immense, spreading across the floor like a dark red throw rug. Yet, as the doctor hovered over the man, he thought he heard the slight sound of breathing. Gordon elevated the passenger's head onto his lap to prevent him from drowning in his own blood. Cradled in Gordon's arms, the blind man opened his eyes.

Doug gazed about at the bizarre scene surrounding him. He was looming just above the ground, poised a few feet away from what appeared to be an aircraft that had been sheared in two. From this elevated vantage point, he could clearly see into the wreckage and was aghast at the devastation found there. His attention was irresistibly drawn to a pair of men ensconced in the rubble. Both were on the floor, one lying on his back, the second bending over the first. Doug was certain he knew both of them, yet couldn't identify them.

Although the situation was certainly odd, Doug was not frightened or put off. He felt quite peaceful, content and relaxed. A sense of euphoria drifted through his soul. He looked away from the wreckage. An even more astonishing, yet equally undisturbing, event was happening alongside him.

Silver white, transparent stairs were taking shape mere inches from his feet. They glowed with a frosty, luminescent light. A first step took form, followed by a second and a third. Within seconds, a glittering stairway, tall as the eye could see, was established. On the final shimmering stair, there was Alex, his son. He smiled down at his dad, his beautiful blue eyes alight with love.

Jubilation exploded in Doug's heart. "Alex, oh Alex," Doug cried as he began mounting the stairs, taking them two at a time.

Alex took a single step forward and said, "No, Daddy, not yet, there's still one more thing."

Doug stopped short. The remainder of the vaporous staircase that led to his son vanished. "What? What is it?"

"Go back. You've got to go back; it's not done yet. There's still one more thing you must do."

"But..."

"It won't be long, Daddy. I promise. I'm waiting right here for you." Alex gestured down toward the foot of the stairs and over to the broken plane. "You must do it. Go."

Dejected, Doug turned and retraced his path. Each step immediately disappeared the moment his foot left its nonexistent surface.

Once again, Doug surveyed the wreckage. But now he knew exactly who the two men were. The moment the recognition was made, Doug was back in the plane, lying prone on the floor, gazing up into the face of Gordon Brooks--the doctor he had hated with every fiber of his being—the man he had wanted dead. But now...?

"There's been a plane crash, you've been hurt," Gordon explained in a soothing voice. "An ambulance will be here soon. Please, just try to hold on."

The words barely registered. They were meaningless, irrelevant. Instead, Doug looked deep into the doctor's eyes and far into his soul. And now he knew; he knew the truth.

Gordon Brooks was no child murderer. He, like all of them, was only a victim of the tragedy and sorrow life has to offer. Alex, the victim of a speeding baseball; Doug, the victim of insurmountable grief; and Brooks, merely the victim of his own inability to stand between Alex and death.

With a supreme effort, Doug moved his lips, struggling to form words. The doctor bent closer. "I am so sorry, I was wrong," the dying man whispered into Gordon's ear. Then, with the very last breath Doug would ever take in this lifetime, he implored, "Please forgive me."

A split-second later, Doug was back outside the airplane. The radiant staircase was created anew. Alex was standing at the top, waiting. Without a single glance back at the world he was leaving behind, Doug raced up the stairs. Alex threw himself into his father's arms. They embraced, then turned and ascended the remainder of the staircase secure in the knowledge that they would be together forever.

II

DR. LUCILLE DREXLER HUNCHED OVER her rosewood desk, clutching the latest edition of the Los Angeles Times between both hands. Her wrinkled face was a mask of sorrow and regret. She read, then reread the front page story and scanned the various related sidebars. Then, still gripping the newspaper, she sank back in her padded leather office chair and simply stared at the ghastly photos, a shiver running up and down her back. One graphically showcased the burning wreckage of the plane's fuselage; a second captured the broken tail of the jet perched drunkenly at the bottom of the mountain; while a third showed the fiery ball of smoke that had stained the San Diego skyline for hours after the crash.

Yesterday, she'd sat at this very desk and observed that ink-black cloud first-hand through her office window, but somehow, and she would have never thought it possible, it appeared even more horrific in print.

Her eyes drifted to the fourth picture which was connected to, but set apart from, the others. It was a black and white studio photograph of Shea Lansing. Even with the poor quality of newsprint, she was undeniably breathtaking. Those lovely eyes, brilliant smile and signature dimple at the corner of her mouth. The bold headline "Super Model Killed in Crash" stabbed at Lucille's heart.

The doctor flung the newspaper back onto her desk and swung around in her office chair. Leaning back, she plucked her tortoise-shell glasses from the bridge of her nose and absently massaged her eyes and temples. Then, she gazed out at the sky above the city through the green and white pinstriped curtains framing the office window. It was vivid blue and clear now, retaining no trace of yesterday's devastation.

Although she'd only met Shea once, Lucille had taken to her immediately. A sad smile swept across the doctor's fleshy face, recalling the way Shea had looked when telling of her virginity. The young woman had actually blushed. *How long had it been since the doctor had seen anyone blush; even more germane, how long had it been since she'd heard anyone admit to being a virgin?*

With no children of her own, Lucille had treated more than one female patient as the daughter she'd always wanted. From the moment they met, she had intuitively believed Shea would probably fall into this category. The doctor had happily anticipated having the opportunity to care for, and care about, Shea for years to come. But evidently, it wasn't meant to be.

Of course, Lucille knew now, it wasn't meant to be anyway, plane crash or no.

She swiveled back to her desk and fished out Shea's patient chart from a sprawl of manila folders on the blotter. Just this morning, the results of her blood work had come back from the lab. As always with celebrities, the blood had been submitted under a false name. Opening the chart, the doctor perused the information a second time. As expected, the tests had confirmed what she had initially suspected. The tip-off, of course, had been Shea's surgery in Africa. Until recently, that particular area of the world had just been unreliable--not a good place to have an operation, to say nothing of a blood transfusion.

The experience in Africa in tandem with the symptoms had led Lucille to an obvious conclusion that she needed only one test to confirm. And there it was, plain as day on the papers before her: Shea had HIV.

Lucille ruminated on the myriad patients she'd already lost to this dread killer, recalling the agony and torment each had experienced during the final weeks and months of the illness. It would have been no different for this young woman. And now she was dead.

The doctor stared at the test results splayed out on the desktop before her, seeing nothing. *Was this horrific, yet instantaneous death really a blessing in disguise, at least for Shea, if for no one else?* She shook her head as if to snap herself out of the dreamlike trance. A blessing? She shrugged in resignation. Maybe, maybe not; she'd probably never know. But one thing she did know for certain was that the facts concerning Shea's medical condition were going to die with her.

Mind made up, her eyes flashed with conviction. "I'll be damned," Lucille unconsciously muttered aloud as she snatched the incriminating lab reports from the chart. Yes, she'd be damned all right if the press was going to get a hold of this information and besmirch the name and reputation of such a lovely and innocent young woman. And she'd be double damned if those filthy tabloids would ever have the opportunity to whip up a bunch of lurid sex-tales about someone who couldn't even defend herself.

It would have been different if Shea had not been killed in the explosion. If the model had died on the ground and survivors had been exposed to her blood, then as a physician, Lucille would be obligated to tell of her condition. But that had not been the case. Shea's body had been incinerated, destroyed by fire. The disease had died with her.

Grunting slightly, the rotund doctor leaned way over and snagged the edge of her trash can with the tip of one finger, then yanked it across the deep green carpet closer to her chair. A satisfying ripping sound knifed through the silent office as Lucille systematically tore every lab report into tiny pieces.

"There," she murmured, tossing the final few shreds of paper into the receptacle. They fluttered to the bottom like falling snow. The information was now destroyed, reduced to nothingness--not unlike Shea Lansing herself.

III

CONNOR LET HIMSELF INTO THE silent house and switched off the security system. Turning, he recognized a familiar thump in an adjoining room. A second later, Clyde came tearing around the corner, tail lifted high, dark whiskers swept forward in excited expectation. Seeing the man, he emitted a small squeak and skidded to an abrupt stop on the tile floor, his entire body seeming to droop. "Sorry, Buddy, it's just me," Connor told Clyde in a hoarse voice. Disconsolate, Clyde swung around and retraced his steps back to the hall.

Connor gazed around the foyer as though actually expecting to find something there. Nothing happened. He moved forward and entered the kitchen.

Spying Clyde munching his cat chow, he ambled to the counter.

The man parked his elbows on the tile surface and watched the cat eat. This was what he was supposed to do. Connor had seen Shea go through this routine dozens of times during the past months. He leaned on the counter, observing the cat, mind blessedly blank. Since Clyde wasn't genuinely hungry, just adhering to an established ritual, the cat soon quit eating, leaped to the floor and left the kitchen.

Connor wandered aimlessly from room to room, looking around, touching familiar items. Everything was the same as he and Shea had left it the morning he drove her to the airport. Everything was exactly the same, yet nothing would ever be the same again.

At last, he was in the master bedroom, poised in the doorway of Shea's huge walk-in closet. Detached, he took in her hats, clothes, shoes, inhaling the lingering scent of her perfume.

He stepped forward, extended a hand and ran his fingers up and down the sleeve of a silk blouse. It was one of his favorites. The sea-green hue always caused her exquisite eyes to appear even more vibrant than usual. He raised the cuff and pressed the filmy fabric to one cheek. Shea's familiar fragrance was even more pungent now.

Connor remembered the last time he'd seen Shea wearing this particular blouse. They had gone to dinner with friends; she had been so joyful, so full of life. An expression of the most infinite sorrow crossed his face and then was gone. He let the sleeve drop and walked out of the closet.

Moments later, he found himself sitting on the foot of her bed, hunched over, clasped hands dangling between his knees. He had sat in this room just like this more times than he could count, talking and laughing with Shea as she stood before the bathroom mirror, styling her hair or applying makeup. Now he gazed at the exact spot where she used to stand. He saw nothing, nothing at all.

Shea was gone.

His face, already strained by exhaustion, contorted with pain; yet, no tears seeped onto his cheeks. There were no tears left to cry. Eyes closed, he massaged both temples.

Clyde appeared in the doorway, cut across the peach-colored carpet to the bed and hopped up. He padded across the white eyelet cover and drew alongside Connor. The cat peered quizzically into the man's face, then butted him on the upper arm with the top of his little head. Clyde waited expectantly. Getting no response from the inert man, he butted him again, this time with more force.

Connor finally noticed the cat. He reached out and stroked Clyde's soft black fur. "I'm so sorry. I just can't bring her back," he whispered as the animal circled once, then flopped onto the bedspread with his back pressed against the man's thigh. Connor sat still for the longest time, welded to the edge of the bed, one hand resting on the cat's back. Eventually, he rose and left the room. He went to the office and settled himself in the high-backed gray leather chair behind the desk. For the next hour, he retrieved all the files and important papers he could find in the desk's many drawers.

The previous afternoon, he had spent several hours with Shea's attorneys. The group had reached several critical decisions regarding the future of her foundation. It was decided that Connor would head up the organization. He would dedicate the next several years of his life to implementing her wishes for homeless and abused children. His first love, photography, would have to be placed on the back burner for a while. This was something he must do.

Only he knew what motivated Shea's deep desire to help children. She had never told the lawyers about her traumatic childhood. Yet, she had told the team all about Connor and their future plans. This had made the task of convincing them that he was the one to head up the foundation far easier than anticipated.

Connor eased the last drawer shut, got to his feet and carried the tall stack of file folders and her computer out to his car. Back in the house, he sought out Clyde. The cat remained curled up on the foot of the bed.

Connor stood in the middle of the room and looked about one final time. He moaned deep in his throat. His vision blurred and tears spilled from his eyes, filling the room with pain. "Oh Shea, how could you leave me? I wanted us to be married. I wanted to spend my life with you. I wanted us to have children. We would have loved them the way you never were. I would have always loved you the way you deserved. God, how can I possibly live without you?"

He shuddered and sank to the carpeted floor, crying in torment. With his face pressed into his cupped hands, the man's entire body shook under the weight of wholesale misery. In time, Connor staggered to his feet and went over to the bed. He scooped up the small cat and held him to his chest, scratching his neck beneath the bright-red collar. "Well, Kid," he said to Clyde in a whisper. "It looks as if you're my cat now. And I've got two new friends at my house that can't wait to meet you."

Connor kissed him between the eyes, then clutching Clyde a bit tighter in his arms, he turned and walked out of the room and out of the house.

IV

THE OFFICER SCRAWLED A FEW final notes, then reviewed the page before snapping the notebook shut. "That's probably all the information I need for right now," he concluded and shoved the ballpoint pen into the breast pocket of his khaki uniform. He turned toward Bill Emmerson, who perched on the edge of a low-slung chair. "So, you'll come down to the station tomorrow and give us an official statement?"

Bill bobbed his head in affirmation. "You bet. I'll be there first thing in the morning."

"Good. We'll be expecting you." The officer shifted his attention back to the man lying in the bed. "Well, unless there's anything else, my partner and I will be leaving now."

Gordon shook his head. "No, that's all."

"Then I believe we'll go have a little chat with your wife. Seems like we've got some unfinished business with her."

The uniformed man angled toward the door with his partner at his side. But before leaving the room, the officer addressed Gordon one final time. "I hope you're up and around real soon. And well, I'm truly sorry about the misunderstanding, Doctor."

Gordon raised one hand in protest. "No, please don't apologize. You were just doing your job. I assure you, the fault was all mine."

After the two officers exited the room, Gordon sighed in relief and tossed an appreciative smile to the two men sitting next to the bed. "Thank you both for coming."

Sid Finster, who sat tapping one foot on the institutional carpet and drumming his fingers on the armrest, spoke up first. "No problem, glad to be here. I think everything's going to be fine, just fine." Then, casting a glance at his gold watch, he jumped to his feet. "Better go. I have to be in court in less than an hour."

"Thanks again for everything," Gordon said.

Sid swung around to face his friend, placed one hand on the top rung of the stainless steel bed railing and gripped tight, the taut skin of his knuckles bleaching white under the sudden strain. "No, thank you for finally telling the truth. You know how I felt about this situation from the very beginning." Anger crackled in his voice as he went on, "I would have defended you if need be, but I wouldn't have liked it one little bit." Sid rocked on the balls of his feet as he plunged his free hand repeatedly through his thick mane of silver hair. "Why it just killed me to think of you taking the fall for that little --" Gordon could clearly discern the word "bitch" forming on Sid's pursed lips before he snapped his mouth shut and flushed.

"Couldn't agree more," Bill concurred as he stood and joined Sid. "I've been beside myself for weeks over this."

Gordon considered his two old friends from his prone position on the bed. Their faces, always so strikingly dissimilar, now bore an uncanny resemblance to one another. Each was defined by deep lines of worry and fatigue etched into the brow and bracketing the mouth. Their anxious eyes and pallid skin also testified to the strain each had been under. Gordon thought of the anguish he'd caused his dear friends. And for what? To protect Alyssa, a woman who couldn't hold a candle to these two when it came to character, moral integrity, and especially, love for him. How could he have been so blind?

Sid shrugged into his jacket and straightened his cuffs and tie. Then, struck by an idea, he circled the foot of the bed and went over to a host of festive floral bouquets arranged beneath the room's only window. Sid surveyed the vivid blossoms, then plucked an enormous red carnation and stuck it into his lapel. He fluffed its spiky petals with his fingertips, clearly pleased with his selection.

"Clashes with your suit," Gordon observed.

"This...this from a man wearing a white dress with his ass hanging out the back? And you know 'what' about fashion," Sid retorted amiably and came back to the bed, stooping to retrieve his briefcase from the floor. "Listen," he told Gordon, slapping the side of the case against one leg. "If the police want anything else, just have them call me."

"The minute I get back to the office, I'll start preparing the divorce papers. Although I usually steer clear of divorce work, for you, I'll gladly make an exception. I think its high-time you got rid of..." The attorney paused, a faint pensive frown creasing his forehead.

Gordon could tell he was wrestling with a decision. A second later, the frown disappeared and he completed his thought, "that contemptable bitch."

"Hear, hear," Bill chimed in, clapping his hands together in mock applause. Sid flashed Gordon a thumbs-up sign, said goodbye and bolted from the room.

The door whispered shut as Bill commented, "Honest to Christ, just being in the same room with the guy wears me out. Can I crawl in there with you? I think I need a nap."

Gordon chuckled in agreement, then turned toward Bill. "I honestly had no idea you both disliked Alyssa so much."

Bill scratched his balding head, then inspected his brown leather shoes for a while. He shrugged. "You were married to her. Not much we could do."

Gordon, noting his friend's obvious discomfort, replied, "Yeah, I understand."

A silence settled over the room until Bill declared, "Well, better get out of here and let you get some rest."

"I appreciate you talking to the police ... telling them what really happened that night."

His friend's relaxed expression gradually metamorphosed into one of extreme seriousness. He hitched up one hip and eased onto the side of the bed, careful to avoid jostling Gordon's legs, encased in thick white plaster beneath the hospital sheets.

Uncharacteristically, he reached out and clutched Gordon's hand, gripping the fingers tight. "Look, I'd do anything for you, I hope you know that. Next to Sally and the kids, you're the most important person in the world to me – you always have been. Guess I should have told you that a long time ago..." He paused and cleared his throat. "When I heard you were on the plane that went down, well..." Bill's voice broke. After a moment, he sniffed and spoke again. "Anyway, all that matters now is for you to get better and put this stuff with Alyssa behind you. It's been a nightmare. Time to move on."

Gordon only nodded, knowing no words could get past the huge lump formed in his throat.

After Bill left, Gordon lay on his back motionless, hands folded on top of the pristine white sheet, head propped on the spongy pillow. He was oblivious to the familiar pulse and hum of the hospital surrounding him: nurses chatting to one-another as they strode briskly from room to room, the kitchen staff delivering lunch trays, and the PA system he'd always listened to so diligently for his own page. Instead, a thousand conflicting thoughts tumbled through his mind, the majority revolving around Alyssa--the admission of his own innocence to the police and the decision to go through with a divorce. At this very moment, the two officers were on their way to confront her with the truth. Yet, to his distinct and extreme astonishment, he felt absolutely no guilt, shame or remorse. In fact, if he could magically turn back time and cancel out the previous two hours spent with the police, he would not do it.

Gordon stared trance-like at the sunlight leaking into the room through the slatted edges of the vertical blinds. He contemplated the extraordinary changes that had occurred. In fewer than forty-eight hours, he had been liberated from the ignominy of an arrest, the probability of a future manslaughter conviction and the grip of a destructive marriage. All due to a tragic, devastating plane crash that had claimed scores upon scores of innocent lives. Yet, for him, the event proved to be an actual Godsend.

The doctor considered this mystifying situation. *How could it be? So many dead and him alive.*

His thoughts returned to the man, the blind man who had died in his arms. Gordon had witnessed death dozens of times, and yet there was something about this specific situation that continued to trouble his mind.

He couldn't get over the nagging notion that he actually knew this person--they had met sometime, somewhere before. However, he just didn't know where or when. Even more disturbing, Gordon knew the man hadn't been blind at all. Why he'd looked directly into Gordon's own eyes, there was no doubt of that. But why the seeing-eye dog and dark glasses? And then there were those enigmatic words spoken just prior to his death, asking Gordon to forgive him. Forgive him for what? The question spun round and round in his mind like a moth circling a candle flame.

The doctor squeezed his eyes shut and massaged his forehead, trying to make sense of it all. But he just couldn't. And somewhere deep in his soul, he knew he never would.

Gripped by a sudden sense of urgency, Gordon swung his hand over to the table and fumbled the phone from its hook. He placed a brief call, then settled back to wait. In less than five minutes, the door arced open and Angela Harrison rushed to the bedside, leaned over and gave him a careful hug. "Gordon, thank you so much for calling."

She extended one leg behind her and wrapped a foot around one of the chair's metal legs. Yanking it closer to the bed, she sat down. Angela took his left hand into hers with great tenderness. "How are you feeling?"

Gordon smiled over at the woman, touched by the deep concern suffusing the planes and contours of her gentle face. "I'm doing okay, not too much pain."

"I'm so glad to hear that." She darted a swift glance toward the lower half of his body, then turned full attention to their clasped hands. "I'm so sorry about what happened to your legs, but thank God your hands weren't hurt."

"I agree. And all the doctors say I—"

Angela popped up in her seat, the look of concern instantly shifting to one of real joy. "I know, Dr. Rankin said you're going to be fine, probably be able to walk again in only a few months."

Gordon lifted a questioning eyebrow. "You spoke to him?"

Angela beamed. "Yes, of course, to the entire surgical team; in fact, several times." Embarrassed, a crimson blush stained her cheeks. "Actually, I was there for the surgery and stayed with you throughout the night in recovery. I knew you wouldn't remember, but I just couldn't bear to leave you there all alone."

Gordon knew both of them were recalling Alyssa's noticeable absence. "Angela," he murmured, touched anew by her dear heart.

She leaned closer and gazed down into his face. Now, even Gordon could see the love pouring from her eyes, something he had failed to see for so long. "Oh God, I was working when the crash happened. I was in the ER helping out when ambulance after ambulance pulled up with mangled bodies, mostly dead. And there were so many body parts...arms and legs, headless torsos, blood everywhere. It was impossible to tell what belonged to whom. Then they brought you in and it was, it was..." She started to cry and dropped her forehead onto their entwined fingers.

Impulsively, he reached over and stroked her hair, trying to lend comfort. "Please don't cry," he implored. "It's all over now and everything's going to be fine."

In the following minutes, he told her about his recent meeting with the police. She raised her head and interrupted only once to assure him she'd always known he was innocent of the hit-and-run charges. As Gordon completed the story, he scrutinized her appearance. Her eyes were puffy and red-rimmed and her skin was blotchy from crying. Gordon thought she was far lovelier than Alyssa, with all her youth and beauty, could ever hope to be.

"So all of that terrible mess will soon be over for you?"

"Looks like it." He remained silent for some time, collecting his thoughts, then forged ahead. "Angela, there's something else I want you to know. I'm going to divorce Alyssa right away."

She canted her head to one side. "You are?"

"Yes, and I wanted to talk to you about it. Well, not exactly about the divorce, but about something related...well not really related, but. Lord, I'm making a muddle of this."

She placed a hand on his forearm. "Take your time. I'm not going anywhere."

He smiled at her in gratitude. "After the crash, when they were taking me away in the ambulance, all I could think about was, well, you. Not my life, my work, certainly not my wife-

- just you. It was the most uncanny thing. Not until after the surgery, when I was fully conscious, did I have an opportunity to consider what that meant."

He swiveled his head on the pillow and now the love so recently seen in her eyes was reflected in his. "Three years ago, I was the worst kind of fool. But surviving that plane crash has made me realize that, not only are some mistakes rectifiable, but that you are the woman I always wanted and needed in my life."

At these words, Angela drew in a sharp, startled breath.

Undaunted, Gordon went on, "So, I guess what I'm trying to say is, when my divorce is final, would you consider starting over with me, please?" When she didn't answer immediately, he grew flustered and added, "I don't mean you have to marry me or anything, at least, not right away. I just meant maybe we could date, well maybe not date, that sounds kind of silly at our age, but—"

Angela reached over and pressed the fingers of one hand over his mouth. "Hush, you're babbling." His lips curved into a smile beneath her touch as she said, "Like I said, I'm not going anywhere and the answer is yes: yes to everything. Yes to dating, rendezvousing in the supply closet, shacking up, marrying, anything you want."

Angela looked away and then back, a contemplative expression flashing across her face. "Gordon, I love you, I always have. I've loved you for years."

Gordon felt a supreme contentment settle over him. "You do?"

"Always have, always will."

For the moment, they said no more, knowing additional words would be superfluous. Gordon and Angela simply sat still, holding hands, smiling at one another, thankful to have each other.

V

IT WAS DARK, so very dark. This darkness went on and on and on, until time had no meaning anymore. Occasionally, this black void was punctuated by random sounds, but mostly it remained silent. And there were voices, too—some ear-splitting, others little more than hushed whispers. Two, three, even four voices at a time, all too garbled for comprehension.

Light finally penetrated the darkness, fleeting and ephemeral at first, then gradually escalating in intensity. Sunlight? Maybe, maybe not. But he knew warm, inviting light existed just beyond the darkness. This knowledge buoyed his heart.

On some level, he knew to fully embrace the light. He need only to open his eyes. Yet, the man felt strangely reluctant to relinquish the secure darkness for some unknown entity.

Ultimately, the allure of the light won out. He slowly eased his eyes open. The light was shockingly bright, far brighter than expected. Although his vision was somewhat blurred, he still winced, blinking again and again.

John found himself staring at a ceiling, one he was quite sure he'd never seen before. It bore several deep cracks and was festooned with institutional light fixtures. However, before he could make any sense of this, a face insinuated itself into his line of vision. Beneath his folded hands, John's heart fluttered in his chest as he took in the beautiful eyes, turned-up nose and halo of dark hair wreathing the utterly familiar face.

Why, she looked exactly as he had last seen her. She hadn't changed at all. A thrill of sheer joy darted through him; the corners of his slack mouth strained to reflect the jubilation felt inside. But the effort was too great. "Natalie," he managed to whisper, his voice little more than a croak. Then the darkness claimed him once more, pulling him back down, down into its womb-like depths.

Sometime later, seduced again by the light, he reopened his eyes, squinting to avoid the glare. After establishing he was still lying beneath the same strange ceiling, he swiveled his head and discovered metal bars posted mere inches from his face.

"You're awake," came a cry from the corner of the room, followed by the thump of feet striking the floor and rapid footsteps approaching the bed. Once again, Natalie loomed above, except this time, it was a different Natalie. John struggled to understand. There were the same eyes, hair and smile, but this one looked softer, wiser...older. Yet the confusion this conundrum engendered was eclipsed by the pressing need for an explanation. *Where was he; what was going on?*

Fortunately, Natalie gleaned this need for knowledge and rushed to fill him in. She told him of the plane crash, the severe concussion and other injuries he'd sustained, the subsequent surgery and the days he had spent comatose here in Mercy Hospital. She hovered close, clutching his hand in hers, pausing intermittently to swipe away a tear or steady herself when her composure slipped.

John tried to synthesize this information. *A mid-air collision with nearly two-hundred people dead on the flight to New York?* Overwhelmed, he shut his eyes and concentrated hard, wanting, somehow needing to remember that pivotal day. He could vividly recall traversing the length of the San Diego airport, even picture himself standing in line to board the plane, then, then... As if he'd run straight into a brick wall, he drew a complete blank. *Surely there was more, there had to be.*

Determined, he pressed on. He conjured a mental picture of his seat near the rear of the plane, and yes, now he remembered the little boy with the coloring book. John's eyes snapped open; he blurted out in a raspy voice, "Jeffery, is he okay?"

Now Natalie mirrored his confusion. "Was he on the plane?"

"Yes, a little boy sitting next to me. Did he make it?"

She shrugged, her expression reflecting little hope. "Probably not, so few people did, but I can certainly find out."

Although he tried to remember more, he just couldn't. Only snatches of memory, like individual photographs in an album would pop up here and there--a purple crayon, a flight attendant's uniform, a black dog -- but each individual snapshot was too fragile, too fragmented to piece together into a complete picture.

Natalie spoke again. "I remember talking with you about Shea Lansing. Did you know she was on the plane?"

"Shea? No...no, wait...I saw her get on right before we took off. Is she okay? Is she here in the hospital?"

She shook her head. "Everyone in the front of the airplane was killed immediately."

"Oh dear God, I just cannot believe this."

John noticed Natalie acknowledging someone else on the opposite side of the bed. He turned to see who it was. And there she was, the other Natalie, the one he'd seen first.

Natalie turned back to him and explained, "Johnny, this is Elizabeth. Both of us flew out here the moment we got news of the crash. Because of the situation, I've told her all about us. She knows that..."

But John heard no more. He just stared into the face of his child, the daughter he'd never met until this very moment. She was lovely, virtually a carbon copy of her mother at the same age. But did he see a flicker of himself there too, maybe just a little? Perhaps in the arch of the eyebrows, or the curve of the lips? His own lips broke into an enormous grin, now more than capable of manifesting the delight he was experiencing.

Elizabeth returned the smile, hesitant at first, but ultimately as big as his. She reached out a hand and tentatively touched his forearm and said in a diffident voice, "Hi, Dad."

The simple monosyllabic words instantly closed the gap of time and distance that had separated them. They washed over him, drenched him, consumed him as no two words ever had before. They danced round and round in his mind, then whisked away to his heart where they burst to life like fireworks.

Suddenly, the feeling of loneliness, the sense of desolation and emptiness that had plagued him for so many years, vanished. His heart felt full, full to overflowing as he placed his hand over his daughter's. His eyes welled with tears, their images going temporarily vague. Unable to speak, John just looked back and forth between Natalie and Elizabeth, two words of his own creation now joining and melding together synergistically with those of his daughter: *my family*.

VI

THE YOUNG WOMAN SAT ALONE at the edge of the water, staring out at the curling waves. She wore denim shorts and a pink T-shirt with blue piping around the sleeves and collar. The ocean breeze blew her long dark hair back from her face, which was void of makeup. The setting sun, hovering above the horizon like an enormous gold coin, caused her shadow to stretch out for several feet behind her.

Amorous couples, huffing joggers, and clusters of exuberant children passed by. All unknowingly cut a wide swath around this woman as if her private grief was somehow a tangible thing--something they could touch, taste and smell--something they might catch if they got too close.

After a while, a lone man also dressed in T-shirt and shorts, slowly limped to the woman. He dropped a light jacket onto the sand and placed a hand on her shoulder. Startled, Mandy's head jerked sideways and a smile temporarily broke through the mask of misery. "John, thank you for coming. I'm so glad you're here." She rested her hand on top of his and squeezed with affection.

Not wanting to lean too much of his weight on her, but desperately needing the support, John eased into a sitting position alongside her. Pain flared up his spine and he grunted.

Concerned, she gave him an anxious look. "Your back still hurts."

He gave her a brief nod, pain still carving deep lines into his face.

"I'm so sorry," she commiserated, then on a lighter note remarked, "But I see your hair is growing back nicely."

John fingered the side of his head where he'd been shaved clean prior to surgery. "Back to new in no time. And the pain really isn't that bad. It gets better every day." Pivoting, he gave her bare knee a friendly pat. "Hey, I never got to thank you for visiting me in the hospital. I really appreciated it."

Again, a wistful smile lifted the corners of her mouth. "I enjoyed meeting Natalie and Elizabeth; both of them are wonderful. Are they still here?"

"No, they had to get back. I'll be joining them in just a couple of weeks, as soon as the doctors say it's okay."

"So you're moving there for good?" Mandy scooped up a handful of course white sand and sifted it through her splayed fingers.

"Yeah, I'm hoping to get some kind of work there and live close to the two of them. Natalie and I are going to take it slow, no rush, and see how things work out."

Mandy gave a soft laugh. "You may have every intention of going slow, but I saw how the two of you look at each other. I peg you for married in less than one month. Promise to send me an announcement?"

John looked abashed. "If there's anything to announce, you'll be first on the list. She's pretty special, isn't she?"

"Both of you are special."

Grimacing at another stab of pain, John rearranged himself on the yielding sand. The two remained silent for several moments, appreciating the shimmering sun as it slid deeper and deeper into the ocean. All at once, Mandy declared, "I just wish I understood." John knew exactly what she was referring to and felt a rush of empathy for her as she elaborated, "I wish I knew what he was doing; why was he going to New York in the first place and why the altered appearance. Thank God Doug had his wallet with his license and post office employee card, or we would never have known. But why the rest? You know, after I made the identification, they gave me all his personal affects since there was nobody else but me."

Mandy turned fully toward him. "John, they told me he was carrying a gun."

John winced again; this time it had nothing to do with physical pain. Only recently had he learned Doug Sanders and Gordon Brooks had also been on the New York flight. So he really was going to kill the doctor, after all-- and probably that very day. And now Doug was dead and Brooks, like himself, was miraculously alive.

John dragged a hand down his face. All the pieces of the puzzle had finally come together. Yet, he would not share this revelation with Mandy. What would be gained, besides more pain? Whereas not knowing the truth was certainly difficult, knowing that the man you loved was capable of cold-blooded murder was worse. "I wish I understood, too. But I guess we'll never know. Honestly, Mandy, maybe it's better this way."

"Maybe."

Then, as if in unspoken agreement, she got to her feet and helped him up. The two walked out onto the little jetty protruding from the shoreline. From within her canvas bag, Mandy drew out a small pottery urn and took a few paces forward. She glanced back over one shoulder and said to him, "I know you're not an official priest anymore or anything like that, but while I'm doing this, will you please pray?"

John stood on one jagged rock, stooping to accommodate his back. "I was always planning to."

So, as Mandy edged out along a single outcropping, the former priest prayed, prayed fervently for all of them: for Doug and Alex, for Shea and those who loved her, for all who perished in the plane crash, for those who survived. But most of all, he prayed for Mandy. She had witnessed too much death in too short a time and now had no other recourse but to go on living.

He watched as she sprinkled out the contents of the urn. Most of the ashes fluttered down into the undulating aquamarine water, while others were whisked away by the gusting wind.

Task completed, Mandy stood stock still, staring out at the foam-capped waves. With the now-empty urn clutched between two hands, she bowed her head. Her quivering back testified to the fact that she was crying. Eventually, she turned and looked imploringly at John, tears streaming down her anguished face. "I hope that's what he would have wanted. It's what we did for Alex. Not so long ago." She stopped, pressed one hand to her face, her chest heaving. He could barely hear her final statement. "I guess they're together now."

Her words pierced his heart like a flaming arrow, galvanizing him to go to her, despite the slippery terrain. He picked his way along the wet rocks and she fell into his open arms. Mandy cried in huge convulsive sobs for the longest time. John held her tight, murmuring comforting words she couldn't hear, his own tears dropping onto the top of her head.

The sun vanished behind the horizon. The beach was left awash in soft twilight hues. In time, the two gained enough strength from one another to go back down the jetty. They wandered over to where they'd sat, picked up their few remaining items, then left the beach.

Above, high in the sky, quite unseen by John and Mandy, two white seagulls with black and gray flecked wings circled round and round in the air. One was large with an impressive wing span, while the second was far more diminutive, yet with seemingly boundless energy. In tandem, they dipped low, skirted the jetty where the man and woman had so recently stood, then soared high once more, both issuing piercing cries. Then, one by one, each gull wheeled and winged away, the large bird seeming to set the course, the smaller following close behind.

They flew until both birds were little more than smudges, mere specs of ash on the darkening horizon.